FOR MY CHEROKEE GRANDFATHER,
ROY IVORY VANN, 1904–1991,
WHO HUNTED EACH YEAR ON
GOAT MOUNTAIN,
AND ALL HIS ANCESTORS, INCLUDING
CHIEFS DAVID VANN, JAMES VANN, AND
JOSEPH VANN

GOAT MOUNTAIN

A grandfather, father, son, and a family friend set off on an annual trip to their hunting grounds: 640 wild, idyllic and remote acres along one side of a mountain. But all is not as it should be. Upon arrival, they spot a poacher lurking by their cabin. 'Come and take a look,' the father says. His son peers through his rifle scope until he spots the man, then steadies his breath and lines up the crosshairs . . . Set over the course of one hot and claustrophobic weekend, *Goat Mountain* is the story of a family struggling to contend with a terrible crime, its repercussions, and the slow descent into hell. . .

DAVID VANN

◆

GOAT MOUNTAIN

Complete and Unabridged

ULVERSCROFT
Leicester

First published in Great Britain in 2013 by
William Heinemann
The Random House Group Limited
London

First Large Print Edition
published 2014
by arrangement with
The Random House Group Limited
London

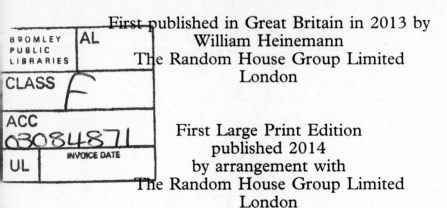
The moral right of the author has been asserted

This is a work of fiction. Names and characters are the product of the author's imagination and any resemblance to actual persons, living or dead, is entirely coincidental.

A catalogue record for this book is available from the British Library.

ISBN 978-1-4448-2111-6

Published by
F. A. Thorpe (Publishing)
Anstey, Leicestershire

Set by Words & Graphics Ltd.
Anstey, Leicestershire
Printed and bound in Great Britain by
T. J. International Ltd., Padstow, Cornwall

This book is printed on acid-free paper

Dust like powder blanketing the air, making a reddish apparition of the day. Smell of that dust and smell of pine, smell of doveweed. The pickup a segmented creature, head twisting opposite the body. A sharp bend and I nearly tumbled off the side.

Kneeling on a mattress tied over the pickup bed, all the camping gear beneath. Northern California, 1978. Gripping through lurches and bends, the metal hot even in morning. Switchbacks up the mountain. I had a shoebox of rocks, and when we hit straight sections of road I'd grab a rock and huck it at a passing tree. The fling and bend, the stone thrown to the side, a thrumming sound, turning and chopping through thick air but swept forward by momentum. Forced off course, bent into an arc, swept forward beyond intent. I had a feel already for that arc, prefiguring it, aiming well behind. Pumping a fist into the air whenever stone bit into flesh. The heavy thud over the growl of the engine, perhaps even a glimpse of bark torn free.

The sky coming down closer, the day heating, the air doubling and doubling again, pressing the smell from all things. Metal, exhaust, oil, dust, weeds, pines, and now a long stretch of dry yellow grass, a valley with sugar pines, a valley that meant we had entered a new land, away from the lake. Every fall this hunt, every fall this return.

We stopped at Bartlett Hot Springs. Pulled over into the momentary twilight of our own dust, my father not waiting for the air to clear, opening his door right away, stepping out a shadow tall and thin, shouldering his rifle. My father etched and luminous even in shadow, a thing set off from the rest of the earth, overly present. Walking away now, up the trail toward the springs.

From the other side of the cab, my grandfather stepped out carrying the lemons, and then my father's best friend, Tom, who had been crammed in the middle, always there from my earliest memories, same as family. Wearing glasses that caught a reflection as he looked up, even in this oblivion of dust. We're here, he said.

I hopped off my father's side of the pickup. Reached into the cab, behind the seat, for my own rifle, a .30–.30 Winchester lever-action carbine with a peep sight, cold metal, not yet heated by the day. No shoulder strap, so I carried it in my hand as I walked up toward the springs. The way I had been and always would be, I thought, hiking with this rifle low in my right hand, barrel tipped downward. Tilt of a needle, that rifle, tilt of the planet itself, sending me forward.

Bartlett Hot Springs long closed, decades before, gated and fenced and abandoned. A leftover from an earlier time. The trail a back way in, narrow pathway through chunks of gray rock embossed with lichen black, orange, green, and white, small wheels and gears and rosettes for telling futures and recording all past. The world stamped onto the world, repeating itself endlessly.

Low branches, dead and snapping against us. On the lookout for rattlesnakes. But the path short enough, and soon we were on a kind of terrace. Old lawn overgrown by grass and weed, old concrete cracked in discrete chunks, vast areas overrun. An enchanted place for me, and only for me, because I was too young to remember, and so in my mind this place could become more.

Women in sun hats, lace and frill, men in multilayered coats with watches and canes. Come to this haven to bathe in the springs and drink from them. This was how I imagined it, and my family somehow a part of that, older and grander. There would have been music, a band in a gazebo, and lanterns hung from the trees at night. Old oaks in here, thick and gnarled but with open space between. There would have been dancing.

My grandfather sat heavy against a low concrete wall overgrown and nearly invisible. A small spigot caked with white mineral. Ready for a taste? he asked me.

My mouth pinching without meaning to. The water would be sulfurous. Yep, I said. My grandfather enormous, a wide inflation of belly beneath a brown hunting shirt and jacket. Always wearing this jacket, even in the heat.

He'd brought a glass, cut the lemon and squeezed two slices as I watched, opened the tap and let the rust run brown then clear. I was always first to taste, and I wondered whether something could have changed since we were last here, the water become poisonous, not only in taste.

Bartlett champagne, my father said, one corner of his mouth in a grin. Long cheeks, like my grandfather.

All three of them watching me now, amused but trying not to show it. The glass filled and sparking in the light, the water moving on its own, the lemon rinds dissolving. Smell of it in the air. Sulfur from deep in the folds of the earth.

I took the glass, cool in my hand, though I'd imagined it warm, radioactive, and I

4

sniffed the top, coughed and regretted that while the men chuckled softly. Then I drank it down fast. The earth's fart, gassed and concentrated through miles of crustal rot and cavern.

Their eyes moist with tears from trying to hold in their laughing, but I could see that. Go on and laugh, I said. I know you're laughing.

My father taken over by it, eyes closed and mouth puckered, but I could see his chest and gut in convulsions beneath his dirty white T-shirt. The squeaky sound of Tom's laughter held back, his face turned away. Sorry, he finally said. It's just your face.

My father put his hand up to cover his mouth.

Like a frog trying to swallow a horse, Tom said, and turned to look up toward the heavens with his lower lip stretched in a grimace.

My grandfather lost it and let out a snort, his belly jiggling as he tied the plastic bag of lemons.

What are you doing with the lemons? I asked. You all still need to take your turn.

My father's eyes squeezed shut with how funny this was, and I saw that no one else was going to drink. Fine, I said, and grabbed my rifle and walked back to the truck.

I climbed up on the mattress and kept my rifle with me, because from here on out, any buck we saw was fair game, and I felt ready to shoot something.

I could hear their laughter up there, but they stopped as they came close, climbed silently into the cab, and we were off again. The wind chill because I was wet with sweat, my T-shirt damp. Palms flat on the cab, rifle pinned under one leg.

Looking for bucks now. Curved antlers in the dead dry branches on a hillside of scrub, or a brown patch of hide standing under a sugar pine, or lying in the shade. Only so many shapes and colors a deer could be, and all the rest was background. Eyes trained to let background fall away, eyes trained to disappear the world and leave only a target. Eleven years old now, and I'd been shooting this rifle for two years, looking for bucks since before I could remember, but this hunt was the first time I'd be allowed to kill. Illegal still in age, but old enough finally by family law.

The world was mostly empty. I knew this already. Most of the land held nothing. A desert. But my father told stories of ducks everywhere on the lake, game everywhere in the woods, and there were photos that showed dozens of ducks laid out, dozens of fish on the lawn, grouped according to size

and type, photos of my father and grandfather and Tom and their friends all posing in
a group with their bucks, two each, ten deer
in a weekend, with good racks. And so it did
seem possible that this desert had once been
populated, and that I had been born too late.
In tens of thousands of years of humans, I
had shown up just twenty-five years too late,
and I was angry about this, even at eleven
years old, angry at my missed inheritance.

The wind hot now, my T-shirt dry, and no
way to know elevation. We were up in
mountains but in a valley, the air hot and
thick. And though I had seen this road every
year, parts of it still surprised me, stretched
farther than I remembered. It would take two
hours to reach our land, and that was a lot of
territory to pass through.

I was a sentinel above the cab, posted for
lookout, but my eyes had dried in the wind,
squinting now, and for miles I did not see a
single living thing other than birds. The birds
were still here. Flickers in low swoops with
wings wide and banded white. Blue jays
and scrub jays loud even over the engine and
tires. All the little brown birds, nameless
and pointless, right along the road. Doves a
pale cream gray, quail running along the road
then flaring. An occasional raptor, sign that
perhaps other things, or small things at least,

lived out in the dry grass. The leftovers. I would kill dove and quail, and after they were gone, I would kill field mice and the little brown birds.

The pickup slowed and we turned down a gulley and onto a beach of large smooth stones. We halted, and there was no dust. The creek low, no more than a foot of water, but fairly wide, at least ten yards. The stones a brightness of color under the water, blues and deep liver red, a break from the yellow grass, brown dirt and bark, green needles, pale blue sky. Richer colors. Glint of fool's gold along the shallow edges, in the sand.

We knelt in the stones, sniffing at the water first, distrusting what might lie dead upstream, but then we drank, cold and clear and heavy. The colder it was, the heavier it became, pressed in close to the stones, running low toward the center of the earth like mercury. Inside each of us now, a downward pull. I was purging the taste of Bartlett and lemon.

Each of us a kind of magnet. I believed that. Each of us feeling some kind of tug. No action inconsequential. Each step taken another step toward an end. I'd known that ever since I'd had memory.

We remounted and drove the pickup through, climbing the bank on the other side, cab and bed twisting, and I was clinging to a

8

small ridge over a side window, feeling the pull backward. Thinking of horses, of a time when we would have crossed on horses, leaning forward in our saddles, low over a mane, and I was bitter I hadn't seen that time. The modern world, all of it, an aberration. Given a TV instead of a horse, a terrible cheat.

The road narrow and low along a hillside, traversing. Stands of trees we passed through then exposed again to the sun. Feel of the air, thinner in the cool sections, fattening up in the light. The day moving on and I was getting baked. Rifle pinned under a leg, but no sign of deer anywhere. Rock and grass and low brush.

The chaparral a kind of blight on the land, thick and unending where no doubt there once had been trees. The bucks lay low in the brush during the day, kept out of sight. Dry brown stalks everywhere, perfect cover for antlers.

The view shortened, the road traveling from pocket to pocket, valleys opening up and closing, but finally we began the long gradual climb along linked ridges that would lead toward the ranch. Views out to other ridges, other mountains in the distance, a sense of the world and possibility expanding.

The road curled along rises and then cut

more deeply into the side of steeper ground. The land falling away to my right, the road narrowing from one lane to less than that, small rocks popping under the tires, and my father slowed, pulled instinctively away from the fall, the tires on the left side on higher ground, the pickup tilting down toward the bottom of a long deep canyon. Slowing to five miles an hour, picking through rocks and bumps.

Up ahead, a slump, land that had caved away and left the road broken. My father slowed and came to a stop fifty feet away. No room to turn around. We might have to back out. I looked at where we had come from, and the track was steep and narrow. Easier ground was far away.

My father stepped out, Tom after him. My grandfather, on the low side, stayed put. Well, my father said. That doesn't look good.

I was feeling vertigo, so I jumped down on the uphill side, holding my rifle. Loose rocks at my feet, sheared and flinty and fresh, a dark gray, no lichen, unearthed recently, fallen from the long scarred hillside above. No vegetation, only ruin. We were driving in scree, traversing a slope of talus, and this had been my nightmare, exactly, for years, driving along the side of a steep mountain with the rock coming down, the momentum of that,

10

unstoppable, though in the dream it was closer to being sand, finer grained, and I was in a school bus rather than a pickup. Still too close to the dream becoming real. I felt what I felt in the dream, that we would be swept away, swept downward to our deaths in the canyon below.

My father put his arm around. Don't worry, all right? We'll be okay. This has happened before.

This was not reassuring, to hear that it was repetitive in real life, just as in the dream.

Tom looking up at the slope above. It's all coming down, he said. Few years, won't be a road here anymore.

My father looked up and studied. Could be, he said. Cutting a new road won't be cheap. But it's Forest Service here. They'd have to do it.

Yeah. What do you want to do?

My father exhaled and puffed his cheeks a bit. Let's go check it out.

So we walked ahead to the slump, three of us single file along the cratered road. About half the width caved away and gone down the hill. Fresh dirt, a darker brown, not yet bleached by the sun. The stone almost black. I was looking at shattered trees below, uprooted, stripped and thrown, the damage continuing beyond the talus slope into forest.

The shock of a boulder flung from hundreds of feet above, crushing at point of impact but radiating outward, cracking of every cell in long pale lines like dominoes. I remember thinking that, as if I could see into the meat of the trees.

Enough room on the uphill side, my father said. The truck would fit there.

Just the angle, Tom said. That's pretty steep.

Yeah. Takes a lot to roll, though.

We could sit on the uphill side, try to weight it down a bit.

Okay.

I looked back at the pickup and saw my grandfather walking toward us along the route we had just taken. He wasn't looking at us, his eyes never looking anywhere, just vaguely ahead. His face showing nothing. Just one foot in front of the other, heavy slow movement that could last for three steps or three days, a walk that could have a destination or not. No glance down at the destruction below. My own grandfather as foreign as a person could possibly be.

The four of us stood there a while, saying nothing, and that was it. No more discussion. I didn't like this at all. We got back in the truck, Tom and I sitting on the uphill side of the mattress, our legs dangling, while my father drove slowly toward the slump and my grandfather remained in the passenger seat. Apparently he was content to tumble down the hill along with two other generations if that's the way it worked out.

Facing uphill, I couldn't see what was happening on the other side. If the tires went off the edge, I wouldn't know until I felt the tilt, and by then it would be too late. I could try to jump, but I'd already be falling through air. Gravity the most terrifying thing in this world, the pull into the void.

My father in low four-wheel drive, moving slowly, rolling at less than five miles per hour. The side lifting as if on a wave, lifting and tilting and I was leaning forward, seeing the wheel well expand as the weight came off the tire, and I didn't know how my father or grandfather would get out in time. They would be trapped in the cab.

I could feel the mountain rolling over beneath us, gravity swinging high in an arc to pull from the side. Gravity a pendulum, and the four of us and this pickup the anchor to that pendulum.

But the side lowered, and the world leveled off, and we had not fallen.

Well that was a little hairy, Tom said. The truck stopped, and he climbed back into the cab. We would have to cross this way again in a few days, though by then the road could have changed.

The men in the cab, me on lookout, and we were high on the flank of a mountain now, an open curve of slope without trees. Only low clumps of brush and dry grass, all other ridges too far away to shoot a buck, so there was nothing to search except the warp of the hill as it was revealed ahead, waiting for antlers skylined and the quick jump and run.

A sunny, beautiful day of blue sky and breeze and birds and our pickup winding toward the gate, which would come just as we hit forest again. I was feeling the excitement I always felt on arrival, because this place was not the same as any other. This was where we returned and had returned for generations. This was what we owned and where we belonged and where our history was kept, all who had come before and all that had happened, and all would be told again during this hunt, and for the first time my own story would be added if I could find a buck.

The last bit of road through cutaway embankments and manzanita, a section I never remembered. And when we emerged, we could see Goat Mountain before us. We entered along the southern flank, a ridge rising to our right past the upper glades and on to steep slides of rock we never hunted.

14

Below this, thick forest, and somewhere in there was our camp and spring and meadow, and below it, the reservoir and bear wallow and lower glades and switchbacks and the burn where a fire had swept through and every other place that had been written into us.

We always stopped here to look, to see who we were. Six hundred and forty acres shared with two partners from the Central Valley. Far away from anything. Divided up in several chunks along the entire side of a mountain, reaching down almost to the edges of the long thin valley below and Cache Creek.

No one spoke. And we could have stayed there looking for any amount of time. But the pickup rolled slowly forward again, the pull of setting up camp, and the track angled down into trees where all views were lost and leaves fallen already from the live oak, smooth dry plates rimmed by spines. Red and green of manzanita. A scrub jay with its harsh call and then an explosion of quail from right beside the road, lumpy brown bodies throwing themselves on low flight paths, wobbling and indecisive, into other brush and trees beyond. I was trained to raise a shotgun and fire, aching now to sight in on those dark topknots as the birds flared their wings for landing. Each of them pausing for an instant, my eye

15

freezing the moment when I would aim and pull the trigger, a moment of perfection, but I was never allowed to kill birds here. No gunfire to spook the deer. And so the quail vanished again into brush and the pickup swept forward and I felt a dull regret. Some part in me just wanted to kill, constantly and without end.

The air cooler now, the road fully shaded, patterns of shadow in the steep slope that fell away to the left. And finally we arrived. The gate ahead thick steel painted the color of dried blood. Heavy pipe construction that no truck could bend, both sides anchored six feet deep in concrete, and a lockbox too thick to shoot. Even a rifle slug would only smear and ricochet. An evolution of gates over the years, and this the final one, put in by my father, a gate that could never be destroyed by any poacher, a gate that would never have to be replaced.

I jumped down and followed my father, who lay in the dirt under the lockbox and reached upward with both hands through a narrow steel chute. This prevented anyone from getting at the lock with bolt cutters or a gun. But there was hardly room for a key, either, working blind and cramped. My father grimacing, his shoulders rising up from the ground. Goddamn poachers, he said. I can't quite turn the key. Get down on the ground behind me.

So I lay facedown in the dirt and gravel and leaves and my father braced against me, raised up, and I heard the lock spring open.

Finally, he said, and he worked a bit more to fish the lock out.

I stood up and brushed off the dirt and leaves as my father swung the gate wide. Tom and my grandfather were standing here now, looking up along the ridge. We got a poacher, Tom said.

I went over next to them and looked up and saw, far away, on an outcrop of rock, an orange hunting vest.

How'd he get up there without coming through this gate? Tom asked.

Must be coming in on dirt bikes, my father said. Too heavy to lift over this gate, but if they follow the main road, there must be some trails now that cut over.

I don't know of any trails, my grandfather said.

Opening weekend, Tom said. Shooting and spooking everything on opening weekend. And why does it matter to them when they hunt? They're breaking the law anyway, so they might as well shoot one in June.

Once they carry it out of here, no one knows where it came from, my father said.

True.

Well let's take a closer look, my father said, and he walked back to the cab. I didn't know what he meant, but he came out with his .300 magnum. He stood and brought the rifle to his shoulder, aimed up at the poacher. A large black scope. It was a beautiful rifle, oiled dark wood. A rifle for shooting bears, too big to use on deer, but it was what my father used anyway, some part in him willing destruction. I had seen that rifle take nearly the entire shoulder off a deer as the bullet came out the other side.

He's a pretty one, my father said. Enjoying a sunny day looking out over all our land and our bucks.

King of the world up there, my grandfather said.

Roll the truck closer, my father said.

So Tom went and released the emergency brake, easing forward to where we'd been standing.

My father aimed again, but this time his elbows were on the hood for balance. He pulled back the bolt and then drove it home, a shell in the chamber. Let's see if he can hear that. I want him to take a look over here and see what's aiming at him.

But the poacher had not moved or looked in this direction, as far as I could tell. He was

18

far away, probably more than two hundred yards, so I couldn't make out his face exactly, but it seemed he was looking down the slope farther ahead.

Tom had his rifle out now, too, aiming up at the poacher through his scope. But I had only a peep sight on my .30–.30.

Come take a look, my father said, as if reading my mind.

So I held the rifle, braced my elbows on the hood of the truck. Smell of gun oil in close, like my .30–.30, but otherwise not the same at all. Heavier and perfect, smooth wood and dark blue metal fused together as if all had been born of one piece, and the balance when I put the stock to my shoulder was perfect too, a thing meant to be and easily become a part of me.

The scope an illumination that seemed without source, a view directly into the world, my own better eye. Texture of rock at over two hundred yards, more than two football fields away. Dark rock with grains and bumps and ridges from weather, a wide slab, and I followed it to the left, to where the poacher sat at the edge, his boots dangling, a rifle lying across his thighs. Jeans and a white T-shirt in the sun, the orange hunting vest. Orange baseball cap. Wanting to be seen. Out here in the open, on our land. He had long sideburns, light brown. His face and neck pink from the sun.

I traced an arm with the center of the crosshairs, moving up from elbow to shoulder. The poacher seemed to sense this, the most uncanny thing. He turned to his left and looked directly at me, into the scope, and he scooted his legs around until he was facing forward. He had seen us, seen something. Some color from the hood of the truck or a reflection on a rifle scope. His hands lifting his binoculars from around his neck and looking straight at me with great dark eyes.

My hand tightened on the stock, and I held my breath. The crosshairs floating just between those lenses. Locked in time with this man, locked in this moment held still.

A slow exhale, careful, as I'd been taught, and I tightened slowly on the trigger. There was no thought. I'm sure of that. There was only my own nature, who I am, beyond understanding.

The world itself detonated from some core and I was flung through the air, landing in the dirt. The aftersound in my ears and pumping of blood. My heart jackhammering. The rifle beside me in the dirt, my right hand still on the grip.

My father lifted me by my shirtfront and threw me backward and I did not hit ground where ground was supposed to be. I'd been lofted past the edge of the road and the earth fell away and I kept falling, hit from behind by a tree trunk or branch and another and another, still falling through air, twisting, and a rush of shadow from the right was all I saw before my right shoulder hit hard in dirt and leaves and I cartwheeled and slammed a trunk with my left leg and was spun around to hit ground with my head and neck and then upright, seeing straight ahead as if I were running down this slope, and I threw my arms out from instinct and flinched sideways to catch the next trunk on a shoulder and was flung beyond bearing until I skittered through leaves and finally lay still, not knowing how I was possible or what would be.

It's rare the world is ever truly new. Rare, also, that we find ourselves at the center. But all had realigned at that moment. When we kill, all that is orients itself to us.

Cain was the first son. The first born of Adam and Eve. Cain is how we began, all who didn't get to start in paradise.

Everything hurt, but it seemed I was only sore, nothing broken. Dark dirt and leaves damp and decaying. Dry on the surface, but I had disrupted the surface. My head was downhill, so I pulled my legs around until I was sitting, and all seemed to work. Legs and back and arms. My right shoulder and legs battered, neck stiff.

A new forest, all trunks very small, nothing old, and that was why I wasn't broken.

Got lucky, I said.

The canopy forming a parallel slope above, just as steep. I was caught between these two planes, the ground that was and the slope above that. A shaftway heading down, a place always in shadow, the sun only a rumored brightness beyond.

The power of that rifle. My legs not braced

well enough. It had blown me flat. I wouldn't let that happen again. That was the way I was thinking. A child's brain is a different thing entirely. What I can't recover is how that brain created a sense of the inevitable, how it connected each thought and movement smoothly, as if they all fit together.

I hiked back up that slope, stiff and sore but still functional. Climbing my way through the trees, each one a handhold and every step of my boots leaving a dark scar in the hillside, the slope that steep that no step held. And when I reached the lip, I found my father and Tom aiming their rifles up at where the poacher had been. My father's elbows on the hood, Tom braced in the passenger door. My grandfather held his rifle, also, standing at the tailgate, guarding the road behind.

What are you doing? I asked.

Waiting to see if someone comes looking, my father said.

You piece of shit, Tom said. You fucking piece of shit. He sounded like he was going to cry. He sounded weak.

I had no scope, no binoculars, so I couldn't see anything up the ridge. It was quiet. Only insects, nothing else. No birds, no wind. The air hot even in shade. My father's white T-shirt wet all down his back and sides and sticking to him.

23

I saw my rifle on the driver's seat. I was reaching in when my father kicked the door closed. I yanked my hand away just in time.

You'll never touch a gun again, my father said.

Yeah I will. I'm killing my first buck this weekend.

My father was very fast. The butt of his .300 magnum heading straight for my chest, but I jumped back out of reach.

What are you, he said.

We have to get out of here, Tom said. Just back out right now and find a turnaround and report what's happened.

He could still be alive, my father said. We have to go check on him.

He's not still alive.

You don't know that.

I saw the shot hit. I was looking right at him in the scope. He's not still alive.

Well we have to go up there.

No we don't. We need to leave.

We're not leaving, my grandfather said. My father and Tom both looked at him, but he didn't say anything more.

Here's what we're doing, my father said. We're driving in around the first bend, out of sight. And we're locking the gate. Then we're going up to check on him.

I'm not going, Tom said.

You're going, my father said. We're all sticking together.

Tom shaking his head, mumbling to himself. He lowered his rifle and walked back along the road, but he stopped after fifty feet and just sat down in the dirt.

My father drove through and came back to swing the gate closed, lay down on the ground to reach up through the lockbox. The tendons in his neck making a trough of his throat. His concentration complete, as if the only task in this world was getting that padlock closed.

My grandfather sitting in the cab, waiting, a thing of flesh with no thought. My father joined him, drove ahead slowly down a road transformed from dry yellowish dirt and spined platelets of live oak to pine needles. A stand of pines on either side, the road more shaded, falling toward a crease in the mountain where a creek ran only in winter. The road red-brown, carpeted in pine straw, the sound of the tires shushed.

I followed, and when I looked back, Tom was following behind me. A figure transformed in a single moment, in that one pull of a trigger. Slack shoulders, head down, rifle held loosely in one hand, a figure refusing to be who he was, where he was, a figure refusing time, also, still holding on to the belief that time could be turned back. Even at eleven years old, I despised him, found him weak, but I was a kind of monster, a person not yet become a person, and so it was possible to think that way.

Somewhere above us, the poacher, and I was eager to see. I wanted time to hurry forward, but every movement was slow, the air itself stagnant. The fall of my boots on this road muffled, the slope on either side indeterminate, shifting, impossible to gauge the axis because some current in my head surged on its own counter-axis.

The truck eased around the bend to the left, riding the shoulder of what would become another ridge, the form of the land generating from itself, and my father rolled to a stop, out of sight now from the gate. He and my grandfather stepped from the cab with their rifles and we met at the crease in the mountain, at the dry streambed.

No conference and no pause but only my father stepping forward into that bed, sound of his boots rolling smooth rocks beneath, and he was carried as if in an updraft, a thing meant to rise and slide along mountains.

My grandfather far slower, a shifting of that bulk at the beginning of every step, a weight that could fall in any direction at any time, no step secure. His .308 over his shoulder on a wide leather strap, his right hand hooked under this strap and pushing at it for balance and steerage.

Tom and I rose past him, up that streambed and then along a slope shielded by pine with only sparse growth beneath, easy to see and move beneath the trees. But then the pines ended and we had to push through brush, Tom raising his rifle over his head, twisting and turning through all that clung and tore. The sound of that isolating us, my father and grandfather gone.

Tom led the way, tall enough to keep his shoulders above, but the branches were in my face and so thick and springy I had difficulty pushing through. So finally I crawled beneath the growth, my chin ducked and face close to the dirt. Eyes closed to avoid being scraped. Knees pushing at the earth, and the sky made of thorns.

Where I was, I didn't know. Tom was gone and all were gone. Movement of lizard and bird, dry shifts of sound. Home of snake and tick and every insect, and no path. No exit on any side, and the sun bearing down. Small dead leaves knit into sharp points. A weight of sound in that heat.

Clinging close to the skin of the mountain, pressing as flat as possible. A thing learned to crawl again. The mountain a heaving presence that could throw us all at any moment. I felt bulky, too large, not well enough attached. I began to feel afraid, and I wanted my .30–.30. I wanted to lever a shell into the chamber and have it ready. I rolled onto my back and held my breath and listened for movement.

Above me layer upon layer of spines. A place it would not be possible to stand. Live oaks as thick as any I'd seen.

I didn't want to move. Any movement would only wrap everything more tightly around me. I was trapped, my heart jerking in my chest.

I did the one thing I knew to do when I was lost. I cupped my hands at my mouth, blowing between my thumbs. Sound of an owl, a hollow sound that would carry.

And then I waited. From high to my left came the answer from my father. And then from farther below, my grandfather. Each of us recognizable, no two sounds alike. And then Tom, from near my father.

I rolled back onto my stomach, pulled myself uphill, no longer lost.

False rattles, insects that sounded like snakes. Explosions of birds. The halting movements of lizards in leaves. I was looking everywhere constantly for the shape of a snake. On the earth above and to both sides and in the low branches that brushed over me. Most snakes I'd seen had been wrapped through branches, just off the ground. Same color but thicker. Baby rattlers no wider than your smallest finger and less than a foot long, looking almost identical to a branch, deadliest because they couldn't gauge their poison yet and had no rattles, gave no warning. I was moving headfirst, so it was my head that would be struck, snake fangs in my forehead or cheek or the back of my neck.

Small movements everywhere, and my fear made me slow. Every few feet I'd stop and look around again. No place I'd ever wanted to be. And I began to think that staying low to the ground was the worst possible way. I began to wonder about trying to get on top of this. But of course I would only fall, ripping down through everything. So I kept crawling.

Hotter and hotter, rising toward noon. My eyes stinging from the salt, all of me covered in sweat, and I heard my father's call, closer now, impatient, and answered back. I had managed to find the worst patch on the entire mountainside, and it was another twenty minutes of crawling before I was out of there. My bruised shoulder and legs stiffening, my neck kinked like it was broken, the fear all through me.

I was able to stand in brush just over my

head, brush that grew like enormous clumps of gray-brown grass but with short trunks beneath. Enough space to push through, and above I could see the rock outcrops. I skirted the base of the lowest one and came up along the far side and found my father.

He was facing away, kneeling and using his rifle as a post to lean against. The barrel in close to his right shoulder and both hands wrapped around it. In his white T-shirt, he was like insect spittle hanging along a stick. The same shape, just as slack, and he didn't turn to look at me.

Tom stood next to him, crucified by his rifle that lay across his shoulders, both arms hanging up over it, hands loose in the air.

They were both looking down at the ground, and I knew I'd find the poacher there. I didn't hesitate, though. Some part of me was not right, and the source of that can never be discovered. I was able to walk up and look at that body and somehow I was not upset by it any more than looking at the carcass of a buck. If anything, I was excited. And perhaps this was because I'd seen so many bucks and everything else dead on the ground all my life. We were always killing something, and it seemed we were put here to kill.

He had landed facedown. Much of the

middle of his back was missing. The hunting vest was still orange up high at his shoulders but had turned red and brown and black everywhere else. He smelled just like a dead buck, exactly the same, and the same large flies had come to swarm around the wound. Iridescent flashes in the sun, black circular orbits bound magnetically to that place, the sound of dozens combining into one, a sound unnaturally loud in all the stillness around.

The rock above had been sprayed, all of it, a swath ten feet long. I understood this was a man, but what I was thinking was that this was an excellent shot. A perfect shot, from over two hundred yards, with a rifle too big for me, a rifle very difficult to hold steady. If this were a buck, everyone would be grinning. There would be hoots and the high battle cry we made only when a buck was killed. We would not be so unnaturally silent. With my buck knife I'd be opening up the belly, then pulling out the innards and eating the heart and liver, and all of that would be considered good. And what if we had never been told that killing a man was bad? Wouldn't we feel the same way then toward a man?

No one spoke. My father and Tom hanging on their rifles and I stood just behind them, empty-handed, and the heat of the day increased. No breeze at all. My shirt burning against my upper back. And finally my grandfather appeared. He walked slightly uphill to a clump of brush and sat down heavily at its base, partly in shade. His rifle across his thighs, the way the poacher had sat.

The flies had doubled in number just in the time we waited for my grandfather. They were drawn as if by an enormous gravity at the center of this man's back. They tried to get away but could not. Every escape bent into an arc that returned. All being pulled down in, the flesh alive now with hundreds of bodies crawling as well as the ones that flew. And we were pulled in the same way, four of us gathered around this man, staring down into that hole.

The flies crawling in short jerks, so that there was never duration, only change. A shifting image, moment to moment and within each moment, but we could never see how or why. I've tried to remember what I saw that day, tried to remember many times, but memory insists on causation and meaning, on a story. Each thing that is leads to the next thing, and there's a reason for that. What I want to recover, though, is that moment in which there was no good or bad but only gravity, and there was no causation but only each moment, separate and whole. Because that was the truth.

My father was the first to speak. That was inevitable. He was the only one with the right and obligation to speak. This can't be told, he said. What happened here can never be told.

The man's dead, Tom said.

I know that.

Well.

Well nothing.

Just leave him, my grandfather said. Don't touch him. Maybe look for the bullet in a tree uphill, see if you can find that and remove it.

My father made a growling sound then, frustration and despair. You're right, Tom. We need to report this. The man has a family.

We're not reporting it, my grandfather said.

He's a monster, Tom said. He's a terrifying little fucking monster. He doesn't even feel bad. He'd do it again.

He was a poacher, I said.

My father turned around to look at me.

You're the one who put the shell in the chamber, I said.

Eleven years old, Tom said. He's eleven years old. This is unbelievable. My daughter is eleven years old.

My father was studying me. The sun so bright I was squinting, having to blink, but his gaze was steady. The buzzing a thousand voices, high and insistent, making each moment a panic.

33

You've ruined the rest of your life, my father told me. Are you old enough to understand that? You may live another eighty years, and every one of those years is destroyed by this.

His eyes a light blue, clear as water, unable to see outward. Sinkholes.

You've ruined my life too, he said.

My father could no longer reach me. He was the one person in this world to hold me in place, but he was powerless. I smiled. It was not something I planned, and it was only a bit of a smile, but there it was.

My father was very fast. I turned and ran, but in a few steps his hand was on my shoulder and he threw me down. Hard earth packed and dry. The small velvet eyes of manzanita leaves. He punched me and did not hold back. For the first time in my life, I felt what he could really do. His fists slapping into me as I curled, covering my head. He was swinging with both arms.

The fist in my back frightening. His knuckles hitting spine, waves of nausea, and I could hear his breath, leaning close over me. If you saw this from far enough away, you might think he was picking me up to hold in his arms, Madonna and child. Saving me from the wolves. But there was no danger from outside, nothing he could protect me against. What we had to fear was inside me,

34

and he was not able to reach that. His fists did nothing. And I think he knew.

My father stopped and lay back in the dirt beside me. I could hear him panting. My body a confusion of pain, my brain unable to sort out where to focus. The air itself hurt. I knew at least not to do anything, not to say anything.

The flies a sound that could not be endured for long, the curve of each flight a distortion of sound, the tone gone lower, and hundreds or thousands of these Dopplers combined made a maw of the air, a growling that came from inside our own ears, without source, and I think it was this that made my father rise from the ground and walk over to the body. I uncurled and saw my father lean down to take this man's hands and his rifle, and he began to drag him down that hillside.

We think of Cain as the one who killed his brother, but who else was around to kill? They were the first two born. Cain killed what was available. The story has nothing to do with brothers.

My father struggled with that body. What to do with it. None of us came close. My father alone pulling dead weight through brush and scrub, over dry ground, walking backward downhill at an impossible angle, hung out over the warp of the earth, held by a counterweight. He paused only long enough to flip the man's rifle into the brush, then pulled the body again.

It's your crime now, my grandfather said. Throwing away his rifle, moving the body. You should have left it like I said.

My grandfather was fifty feet away from my father and not looking at him. Talking as if to the sky.

The flies held still to that cave, erupting at each bump and jolt and settling again. The man facedown, arms held high in worship, head hung low in meekness before his god. Legs trailing behind, slow crawl of a penitent.

36

You're going to be carrying that body farther than the truck, my grandfather said. You're going to carry that body the rest of your life. It will never leave you. You should have left it like I said.

My father having to lunge backward through thick brush, yanking the body. Snap of dry branches and twigs, and the penitent always close behind, following, head lolling, arms raised toward my father and that open blue sky.

All I could do was follow. I followed those tracks exactly. And behind me, Tom.

Only a fool picks up what's laid before him, my grandfather said. Only a fool.

My grandfather had grown up on a farm, told stories of peeling potatoes and adding a bit of extra protein when he scraped a finger. He ran traplines for meat and hides. Even as a kid I had a sense that he had picked up only what was laid before him.

Dragging that body down through manzanita, my father was struggling. I could see he wanted to quit. The flies a berserk horde. The sun directly overhead and his face formed in shadow, dark sockets for eyes, lines in his cheeks, his mouth another shadow. No longer cut out from the earth, no longer the same presence, diminished by this task, the edges of him connected now to air and brush and

37

ground, made real.

I could grab his legs, I said.

Don't touch him, my father said.

Why?

But my father wouldn't answer. He only kept stepping backward down that slope until he hit pine and the body slid easily through needles and the growth was thin, and then he stepped faster, hurrying that body to its conclusion. A kind of sled made of the man, slurring down toward the road. When the slope dove more steeply, my father stepped to the side, swung with all his might, and the body tumbled the rest of the way, rag doll with the stuffing out.

At the road, my father looked toward the gate, but no one had come. Tom helped him now. They each grabbed a wrist and walked toward the truck, dragging the body between them. The man still facedown, the crater in his back still oriented to the sky. He could have been a drunk being dragged home by friends, but metaphor had become literal, the center blown out of him.

Pine-softened road, but at the bend it became rockier, and the man and his clothing were snagged and torn and covered in a white powdery dust. My father and Tom heaved him onto the mattress, swinging him like a hammock, Tom holding the feet. He landed without sound, and I climbed the tailgate to join.

We had to wait for my grandfather. Tom and my father in the cab of the truck, not speaking. The body stretched out behind me, lying across the bed faceup now.

Face of a ghost, white-dusted and blood-less, blue-lipped even in this heat. Eyes gone opaque from dust. Sideburns and hair different than on a living man, become distinct, unrelated to flesh. Mouth open. He could have been sleeping except for those open eyes, the open-eyed sleep of the dead.

I was losing my indifference. I sat back against the cab, but he was only a few feet from me, and he was nothing like an animal. Even in death, his expression was one of wanting more. A disbelief at being ended.

In the center of his chest was one small disruption, a rough dark entry point and a caving from gravity, all the backing gone.

His arms flung above his head, hands open. Shirt and vest dark and jeans dark and legs unstrung. A presence that would stay among us.

My grandfather appeared on the road. Heavy steps, never looking down. A thing that could topple at any moment, but he never looked where he stepped, only gazed blankly ahead, always unconnected to the ground.

And this made any end possible.

No glance as he passed me. No glance at the body. Opened the cab door and heaved himself inside, the bed tilting beneath us and springs adjusting.

Then my father started the engine and we rolled forward as if this were any other trip, same as any other year. Up through a draw and then around a bend and the world opened up again. A long thin ridge fell off behind us to the left, steep slope of pines growing at a sharp angle to the land. A place too steep to hunt. Gray rock and slides of scree among the green, and the bottom of that place gone from view.

The road ahead traversing the mountain. I was on my knees and looking upslope to the right, not wanting to look at the dead man. Wind in my face, my hands low, the top of the cab too hot to touch. I had no rifle, but I looked for bucks anyway, something automatic in me.

That world at a tilt. A sense of elevation, almost the same as flying. And the mountain growing, each part of it enlarging as we approached. Beyond another ridge, an open bowl with only scattered ponderosa pines. Just above us to the right, a reservoir, dammed, lined by trees. I could see its lower bank, heaped up by a bulldozer decades before, covered now in ferns and seeps in that otherwise dry place.

My family had killed a lot of bucks here. An open valley with small rises and only spotty cover for hundreds of yards in every direction, the most gentle part of this mountain. Usually we'd stop and look all around with scopes and binoculars. But this time we drove on.

Side roads heading down to our left, lower on the mountain, to switchbacks and several enormous glades and the burn and bear wallow and another reservoir. We owned this entire realm. It was ours. From this point, we could hike in any direction and not have to cross onto another's land.

I'd like to remember what that felt like, to own and to belong. I've lost the sense of it. I have no land now, and I can no longer visit our history.

We drove through that familiar landscape and believed it would always be ours. It was so certain it was never even a thought.

41

Our camp in a large stand of ponderosa pines, cool and shaded. Always a breeze and the sound of that breeze in the treetops. A spring that ran cold and pure. Ferns and moss and mushroom. Miner's lettuce we could pluck and eat fresh, bounty of the land. As close as we'd know to Eden, as close as we'd come to being able to return.

My grandfather had built small water-wheels here, and several had survived the winter. Turning still in the stream, miniature engines of imagined villages, all built for me, and before that, for my father. Each made from only three small slats and two nails, but animated beyond that. The water shallow and clear across a wide delta of small islands, an entire land, a region twelve feet across, not yet carved into deeper channels or bends, a world too new to have left a mark.

Downstream, at an impossibly larger scale, a pole lashed high between two trees, hooks hanging down by chains, one of them a scale for weighing bucks.

From my earliest memories, all features of this camp had been in place and nothing changed. The spring fed into a black plastic hose that gushed without ceasing into a white basin, the stream three inches thick. Beside this, high wooden countertops, freestanding, for the Coleman stove and griddle and boxes of provisions, Tom's place, the camp cook from before I could remember. All of it open to the pines above and the sky.

Just down from this kitchen, close along the land of the water-wheel islands, a picnic table between two trees and a steep corrugated roof above. The primary structure of the camp, without walls, this open table, the place we gathered, where lanterns were hung and stories told.

And that was it. Off in the trees, generations before me had left old rusty box springs, turned as brown as the pine needles, and farther off, a few pieces of plywood tacked between two trees for an outhouse.

The camp an outpost in an enormity. The slope of pines extending above, gradual at first and then rising much higher along the mountain. We could see only the bases of dozens of trunks as they rose, a contour of land still to be discovered. And below us, the stream curled around and left a fringe of fern and pine and then a wide meadow. Dry yellow grass baking in the sun and filling this forest with light.

All was ideal: the cool shade and breeze, the light, the sound of the stream and pines, the smell of sap and grass and fern, the history and feeling of arrival, of belonging. To me, this was the best part of every trip, the moment we found ourselves here again, the moment all the time between collapsed.

I hopped down from that mattress. I was ready to set up camp.

But my father and grandfather and Tom remained in the cab. There was no sound of talking. They were only sitting there. And when they emerged, finally, they didn't look at me. They gathered at the back of the pickup and looked at the dead man, who lay still with his face to the sky and arms flung above and mouth and eyes open. As if he would take in all the world, all at once.

I'm not touching him, Tom said. I'm no part of this.

I wasn't asking you, my father said.

You had one chance to not be a part of this, my grandfather said. You could have walked back down that road. Not gone through the gate. That was your one chance. Now it's the same as if you pulled the trigger. It's the same for all of us.

That's bullshit, Tom said. I haven't done anything.

What you've done or not done doesn't

44

matter now. Where you are is what matters.

My father grabbed the dead man's hands. Fuck this, he said. And he pulled the dead man from that mattress overboard to whump hard onto the earth and kept pulling and dragging him toward the hooks.

You can't do that, Tom said, but my father kept dragging.

He's not a piece of meat, Tom said.

He is now, my father said, and he dragged across pine needles and the dead man with his open mouth seemed amused and a little drunk, his chin on his chest, and then his head lolled back as if he were laughing. On his way to some new place of hilarity and chains and hooks.

My father dropped him at the base of those trunks, at the edge of the stream. The place all our bucks had hung. He reached up for a dark hook that had several extra feet of chain trailing. Help me lift him, he said.

I'm not doing that, Tom said. He held his rifle in both hands before his chest, barrel aimed upward. At the ready, as if he planned to take aim at any moment. He was one step from panic. I could see he was breathing fast.

It doesn't matter whether you help now or not, my grandfather said. You've already grabbed that man's wrist and helped drag him to the truck.

You shut up, Tom said. I'm sorry. I know I've never said that to you before, sir. But please just don't say anything more.

It doesn't matter what I say or don't say.

Time to do this, my father said.

Tom's glasses made him weaker. The fact that his own eyes couldn't see, the fact that he was always relying on help. And the stock of his rifle was held together with packing tape, a thick brown wad of it, where the stock met barrel. An old .243 Winchester Savage, a light rifle for deer, small caliber, faster but with far less impact than my own .30–.30. It was a gun to be despised, a gun to be ashamed of.

I'll help, I said.

You stay away, my father said. I'll do this myself. He walked over to the trunk where several ropes were lashed. He loosened the one tied to this chain and hook and let them lower to the ground. Then he knelt at the dead man's feet. Work boots, not hiking boots, and jeans. My father lay the hook between these boots and then wrapped the chain around the man's ankles, pulled each wrap tight and then skewered the chain on the hook, anchoring it in place. His face intent, studying his task, a jeweler setting a stone.

Okay, he said, and then he went back to the

trunk and heaved on that rope. The sound of chain links sliding over the crossbeam above. The dead man's feet rising up, legs coming off the ground. He kept his legs straight, cooperating, not wanting to make a fuss.

My father wrapped the rope around the trunk and held it with one hand, used the other to sweat the line. And so the legs of the dead man rose in jerks that caved but each time found him a little higher, until his waist was off the ground and the pale skin of his stomach exposed as his shirt fell away.

Dried caked blood on his skin but the whiteness apparent anyway. An illumination beneath. We were at the edge of that forest, the dry yellow grass of the meadow just beyond us radiating, a brightness that severed that part of the world, and the dead man belonged to that place already. He was not where we found him but could trick the eye. And he was turning now, a slow spin as his shoulders came free.

My father heaved at the line as the weight increased. Hard jerks, and the dead man turned until his back showed to us, the shirt and vest fallen away, and that cavern a dark eye iridescent and moving. His head was free then jammed back into the ground then free again and lifting, and his arms lifting, and he kept turning and we saw again the white luminous belly covered in a dried dark film.

My father heaving backward on that rope, pulling at an enormous bow, facing away from the dead man as if they had separate labors. The dead man's arms swirling against the ground dreamily, mouth open in rapture. And then he was gone to us again and again we saw that cavernous eye in glints blue and green.

Not one of us could speak. I had never seen anything more beautiful. The bright meadow beyond, and the fall off the edge of the world from there, the source of this breeze as the mountain dove and we could see only blank air and other mountain ranges lost in the distance. The dead man in his slow spin before us somehow able to pull that distance toward him and able to tilt even the ground beneath us, collapsing all.

My father had seen nothing. He glanced back only to check that the man's head was high enough above ground, and then he wrapped the rope around the tree several times, careful not to let it slip, and tied off. Get one of the sacks, he said.

It wasn't clear who he was speaking to, but Tom and my grandfather didn't move, so I went to the truck, reached behind the seat and saw my rifle. I put my hand on the stock but then grabbed one of the burlap sacks beneath and pulled it free.

My father was tying the man's arms up to his sides. He tried wrapping, but that was slipping down, so he let the arms fall and tied one wrist, brought the rope up through the man's crotch and led to the other wrist, cinched it tight, the man with one hand at his crotch now and the other at his butt, as if covering himself from view, a modest dead man caught without any clothing, except his jeans were still there.

The dead man's behavior could not be accounted for, but my father slipped that burlap sack up over him and he was lost from view and no longer to be considered. Except that somehow hanging there in a sack like the carcass of a buck he became even larger in my imagination and I could see his open mouth and eyes and his look of pure wonder at the world. His skin had become whiter, and he was taller.

The sack was not long enough to cover his boots. My father kept heaving upward on that sack but it was at its limit. He'd have to tie around the man's ankles or shins, around his jeans where the chains bit in, and these yellow-brown work boots would remain for all to see.

You can't leave his boots showing, my grandfather said.

I'm aware of that, my father said.

Anyone could see it's a man, not a buck.

I get that, Dad, my father said. It's not a brilliant fucking insight you're sharing with me.

We're going to prison for a long time, Tom said. All of us. Except maybe the one responsible, since he's a boy.

How about shut the fuck up, my father said.

Yeah, because I really owe you. You're doing so much for me here. Thanks for being a great friend.

My father knelt down and pulled up on the man's head. Then he looked at me and said, Come here.

So I knelt before the dead man and pulled his head against his chest. The burlap rough, like the weave of tree bark, and the man's face hidden but I knew his mouth would close as his chin hit his chest. It won't matter if you cover the boots now, I told my father. Because he'll only get taller in the night, and then his boots will stick out again.

My father looked down at me, and I could see for the first time that he was not a handsome man. His chin too fatty on an otherwise narrowing jaw, and his nose too bony. His eyes might even have been too close.

My father returned to his work, tying that

50

sack around the chain above the man's boots. Done, he said. And thanks for the help, everyone.

We all stood back and looked at the man hanging there upside down. Even in burlap, it looked like a man. You could tell he had shoulders and his head pinned against his chest. You could tell those were boots at the top. A man learned to sleep upside down, wrapped in rough burlap wings larger but essentially the same as the wings of any other bat. Underneath, a body white as chalk. Waiting for nightfall.

Good enough, my father said. Time to set up camp.

So we pulled at that mattress that was darkened now on top and we carried it to one of the ancient rusted box springs and flipped it over, leaving the clean side to face the sky. This bed was for my grandfather, who had a bad back along with all his other ailments. The rest of us would sleep on the ground.

My father helped Tom carry the wooden crates of canned goods and plates and utensils to the tables beside the sink. They weren't speaking or looking at each other. Tom's face in those glasses could have been a boy's face, someone my age. Dark hair, not receding like my father's.

I hung the lanterns at the table. I carried

my bedroll to a place between the trees where I always slept, level ground and pine needles.

Tom fixed lunch, as he always did. Just bread and lunch meat and cheese set out on the table, ketchup and mustard. We all sat on the benches, my father and grandfather on the uphill side, Tom and I being pulled slightly backward by gravity on the downhill side. The table had never been level.

Each of us with our hunting knives, long wide blades. My grandfather cutting his sandwich into strips like jerky. No place mats, just the stained old planks of the table and our knives etching into the wood as we cut. The blades thick on top, channeled, curving at their ends into narrow points. Each of our sandwiches cut differently, my father diagonal, Tom in simple half, mine in a cross, four pieces. And when we finished cutting, we stabbed our knives into the table so that they all stood on end, four pillars among the lunch fixings. Every time we came here was the same, except this time we didn't talk. No one had anything to say. Cicadas turning the air into clicks and a pulse. Flies, the large horseflies that could take a nasty bite out of wrist or ankle. We moved only to chew or to swat away the flies, and we all looked down at the table.

The pines above us moving in the breeze

and then silent again. The water at the basin. The growing heat in the meadow, radiating into the trees and shade.

Well, my father said, and he rose and walked away to his bedroll farther back in the trees.

My grandfather opened a pack of Saltines and crushed a handful into a tall plastic cup. He poured milk over them and ate with a spoon.

Tom got up without a word and wandered off to his bedroll, and I listened to my grandfather chew. Sopping and smacking sounds. Middle of the day and nothing but the insects inclined to move.

Well, I said, and I walked to my bedroll, an old green army sleeping bag that was too hot to get inside. I lay on top and looked at the pines against a bright blue. All vision moving toward the center, the pines rushing toward the blue but also remaining in place, as if they could constantly shed shadows of themselves, streaming off into the sky but never becoming any less substantial. All the world a kind of vapor drawn from what would not change.

The ground I was on could have slipped anywhere along that mountain, and could have caved in to any depth or seemed to cave. There were four points of us, and a fifth hanging, and all the rest only background.

Why is it that we hunt? Isn't it to return to something older? And isn't Cain what waits for us in every older time?

When we woke late in the day, it was to prepare for the evening hunt. The air freshened, no longer heavy and dead. A promise at the end of every day, a quickening. The shadows of the trees extending beyond measure, smooth dark strips all angled in unison. Each yellow blade of grass in the meadow aligned also, inscribed, etched into existence, and the tallest of the ferns along the creek casting primeval banded markings across a mirror of water.

The breeze in the tops of the pines had increased, and this gave urgency to our movement. My father and grandfather and Tom gathered their rifles and shells, canteens and binoculars, dark jackets and hats. Voiceless shapes in that forest, each grim and intent, awakened from the shadows.

We could have been any band of men, from any time. The hunt a way to reach back a thousand generations. Our first reason to band together, to kill.

I was not allowed my rifle. Weaponless, an outsider on the hunt that should have been my initiation. I was so angry about this I could not have found a way to speak. I climbed into the back of the pickup and waited.

The bed of the pickup cleared out now, and I could stand, my shoulders above that cab. We should have been hiking into the forest, stepping quietly, hidden by trees and looking for antlers or a twitch of ears or a patch of brown lighter than the background. Stopping to listen. But my grandfather had become something modern, an obesity pumped full of insulin and pills and unable to walk through a forest for miles. A thousand generations, tens of thousands of years, ended by him. Having to sit in a pickup and hunt with an engine, loud enough for every buck for miles around to hear we were coming. Unconnected to the ground, rolling on tires that snapped and popped and left a track that was foreign and unimaginable.

I watched my grandfather as he gathered and shuffled, and it did not seem possible that I had come from him. All features fading from his face, receding, leaving only expanses of blotched flesh and wattle.

My father sliding toward that same face, chin and cheeks loose. No word among the men, moving as silently as possible, all absurd since we were about to start the engine. They climbed into the cab with their rifles between their knees and pulled the doors shut carefully, no more than a click for each.

Then the engine, and backing and turning around and we rumbled on down that road, and who cared what the road held. I couldn't even look at it. Pointless hunt. I was the spotter, but I looked instead at the trees. The older forest and then the newer one, the open section of land that had been logged a few years after my birth, all the trees thin and individual, planted, the areas between filled with wreckage. Grasses and ferns and poison oak gone red with fall, looking like bunches of flowers, a junked landscape waiting to burn, all smaller limbs left behind by the loggers and decaying still, choking every pathway, making a false floor.

I pounded the top of the cab with my fist and we lurched to a halt. The doors flew open and Tom was out the right side first, raising his rifle to his shoulder. Then my father out the left side, raising his rifle.

Where is it? Tom said. Trying to whisper but hoarse and loud. Where's the buck?

I pointed to where the new forest rolled downward into brush and a lost part of the ranch we never hunted. We never found bucks this close to camp.

What was he? my father asked.

A big buck, I said. A three-point, I think, but he was leaping and moving fast into the brush.

My father took off across that wasteland at a run. Tom on his right flank and me following. No foothold secure. Small limbs and sawed-off stumps and holes everywhere, but the top of my father floated as if on springs, facing forward exactly to where I'd pointed, looking for that buck. His legs and boots laboring beneath, unconnected.

I looked back and saw my grandfather mired far behind, lost to the chase, and I smiled and tripped and went down hard into poison oak, greasy curse that would puff up along my face and neck and arms within a day, but I didn't care. That was part of every hunt anyway. I was back on my feet and running hard, trying to catch up to the men. I wanted to whoop out loud, because I loved this. If they weren't going to let me hunt, we'd chase phantom bucks into the worst hell this land could offer.

Running straight into the sun, low on the horizon. Tom holding his rifle in both hands, leaping over every obstacle, looking like a jackrabbit. My father lower and smoother, his rifle in just one hand, pulling ahead.

Shape had been transformed into color. My feet looking for the light brown of dirt, flat, avoiding darker shades of fallen branches and the white-gray of trunk tops or dark red rot. The yellow only an illusion, a screen, the same as air, insubstantial. Dry grasses were what we swam through, up to my waist in some places, veering to avoid thistle, milky green and white spines.

The trick was to look farther ahead. You could trip only if you looked too close, if you worried about what was happening right now. If you kept a wider view, staring into that sun, you could never fall.

My father and Tom shadows in that light, half-presences, becoming insubstantial, becoming movement without weight. An arm back, midstride, might catch the sun and the body would become a body again, but then return to shadow that stretched all the way to me and far beyond.

They were moving faster and faster, and I was losing them, falling behind, but then Tom would leap, and the height of his shadow would fling past and over me and the gap between us would collapse. He could expand or collapse and every part of him would remain to scale, and all the while, in every moment, everything around him grew, every long shadow of every thin tree, the world stretching toward me as I ran.

My father a more constant shape, held low, a different gravity. It didn't matter that the buck was imaginary. I knew he would find it anyway. He would make a buck appear. He'd shoot on the run, that big boom rolling out across ridge after ridge and slapping back from the mountaintops.

What we wanted was to run like this, to chase our prey. That was the point. What made us run was the joy and promise of killing.

I could feel my lungs, my legs, but this was only because I knew there was no buck. The men would not feel a thing, all pain washed away in adrenaline. There was no joy as complete and immediate as killing. Even the bare thought of it was better than anything else.

My boots heavy as I lost sight of the men and focused only on the branches and trunks and brush and grass before me, trying not to fall. Fear of snake, fear of twisting an ankle or breaking a leg. I had been knocked out of the dream, but my father and Tom were still there.

I stopped and bent over, my hands on my knees, and tried to catch my breath. Looking back, this seems strange, that a kid could ever tire, but I remember my chest and head pumping and dizzy and everything over-whelmed. I remember walking after that, stepping over all the deadfall, and coming to poison oak so thick there was nothing to do but wade through it. Glossy, waxy green, the edges turned red, as if the plant had poisoned itself, rotting away and dying even as it secreted more poison. You have to wonder why it exists in this world.

Where the forest has been cut, all the most vicious plants grow, each one struggling to choke out every other. Thistle and nettle, live oak and poison oak, burrs and spines and thorns. And this is where I had sent my father and Tom, and this is where I followed.

We pushed our way into this oblivion and just kept going, the land falling down in a slow curve. The sun failing, winking along the farthest ridge and then gone, the sky still bright, the planet turning beneath us. Each of us alone now, separate on that hillside, hearing our own footsteps and blood against the rise of a breeze, the hot air from low in the valley making its way upward.

I did not call out for my father or Tom, and they did not call out for me. We continued, each of us, until that point when the sky had faded enough that we would return at the pickup in darkness, each of us knowing exactly when that would be, and though we took separate paths, we knew we would arrive at the same time.

Walking in a void. The truth of every landscape. When the promise of killing is taken away, the brush is without name, a dozen varieties but all of it dry and reaching upward and compact and unforgiving, grown too close and shortening all escape. The sky new and old and nothing, and the earth insubstantial. We walk on because that's all that's left.

My hands were empty, no rifle. What's good is to hold the grip of a rifle and let the barrel go over a shoulder. The weight of that cutting a crease along your neck. The swing of it as you step, the burden and the heat still in that barrel. And in higher brush, to hook your other hand over the barrel and carry that rifle on both shoulders. You become a giant when you hold a rifle like that. The distance from your shoulders down to the ground increases, and you can wade through any brush and never be held back. And you're still watching for movement to both sides. In an instant, you could bring that rifle down and fire. One foot would be back for balance, but you'd never have thought to put it there. And even if you never find movement and never bring the rifle to bear, still it's the two of you walking in that void, and the night as it closes in feels companionable.

But with no rifle, the air is only air, and it's impossible to know what to do with your hands. Arms up to fend against brush but the hands themselves useless, and the brush grown tall, and no bearing available, one's track winding like a snake's. Buried in brush, and all of it endless, and each step a struggle.

I tore through enormous stands of poison oak and finally was clear to cross that more open wasteland, too dark to see the truck but light enough still to find my way, everything timed to the light from before I was born, and my feet timed, also, and my breath and my blood and even my thoughts, which were of nothing.

We stood around that pickup looking at the ground or the sky.

Too dark to track, my father finally said. But we'll get him tomorrow.

Been a long time since we've gone down through there, Tom said.

Years, my father said. More than that.

Might be nothing down there.

Might be. We can decide in the morning. See how things look.

The four of us darker presences in that night, which had become cold already. The air too thin to hold heat once the sun was gone, but somehow it held still the barest bit of light. Enough to tell that my father and Tom both held their rifles in the crooks of their arms, barrels pointed down. My grandfather's on a strap on his shoulder. A shadow in darkness can move anywhere, and as I blinked or shifted my glance, the men would veer closer or fall away.

Might be nothing at all down there, Tom said.

Might be, my father said. But we've seen one.

He says we've seen one. Did you see one, or any sign of one?

No, my father said.

He was a big buck, I said.

We heard that, Tom said. Outlined in sun, I'm guessing. All ablaze. Every point on fire, and leaping fast through all that crap.

Yeah, I said.

And disappearing just as we looked that way.

Yeah.

Okay, my father said. That's enough.

We've never seen a big buck this close to camp, Tom said.

Doesn't mean we didn't see one now, my father said.

How many years? Tom asked.

Bats were flying over, pieces of the night come loose and diving down between us. No sound of their wings.

What happens now doesn't owe anything to what happened before, my grandfather said.

Yes it does, Tom said.

And what from before told us he would shoot that poacher?

That's not the same.

Sure it is.

The cold sinking down over us. The way we'd stood many times, gathered around the pickup in darkness at the end of a hunt, except there was no smell of sulfur. That was missing.

That buck could be there or not be there, my grandfather said. You have no idea which it is.

It's getting cold, my father said. Time to get back to camp.

All three of you have gone crazy, Tom said. All three of you.

My father opened the driver's door and the light came on. The only light on that entire mountainside, and my father's thin hair as he tilted in. Then Tom scooting into the center with his rifle barrel leaned back against his shoulder, and then my grandfather.

I sat down in the bed, kept low against the cold as the truck twisted and the four-wheel drive moaned, and we were back in camp quickly.

My father fired up the lantern first thing, pumping at it in darkness and then lighting the wicks, like tea bags on fire, and then the flames sucked in and grew white-hot as he opened the valve more, the sound of a furnace, a soft roar.

He set this near the griddle and then made a fire in the pit just before the table. Big Blue Tip kitchen matches and newspaper, smaller sticks and then the split wood he had brought. We sat on log rounds as Tom worked on dinner. The fire grown and the heat coming off it, the three of us leaning in as close as we could. The sparks lifting up into the pines. The fire setting us apart from all else. The first thing to distinguish man. Hunting in a group was older but shared by animals.

There's not much we can do that is older and more human than sitting at a fire. The way a flame surrounds a piece of wood and illuminates, how soft that flame looks, and how it seems nothing at all will happen to the wood. Blond still beneath, visible through flame, and the transformation to black is something unnoticed until it's already done.

No edge of a flame ever breaks or tears. It can take any shape at all, but every change is fluid, every edge rounded, each new wave born of the last and complete and vanished.

65

It's only in fire or water that we can find a corollary to felt mystery, a face to who we might be, but fire is the more immediate. In fire, we never feel alone. Fire is our first god.

We could hunt the glades tomorrow, my grandfather said.

We should go back for that buck, my father said.

You know there's no buck, my grandfather said.

Three generations of us staring into that fire, into the first coals, radiating orange, a deeper color to the heat. The wood organizing itself as it was consumed, segmenting into rectangular coals. And where did this order come from?

You don't know that, my father finally said.

What I know is that he's not right, my grandfather said. Something in him is not right. And what we should be doing is killing him right now and burning him in this fire.

You're talking about my son, my father said. Your grandson.

That's why we should be the ones to take care of it.

Neither of them were looking at me. They spoke about me as if I were a million miles away.

I'd kill you first, my father said.

I know that, my grandfather said.

66

In firelight, their faces two versions of the same, separated only by time. Same eyes staring down into the coals, same hands outstretched, only the surface different. Older skin, and my grandfather swollen and infirm. But if you could cut away the fat, go back in years, you'd find the same man.

What I can't remember is what I understood. I know my own grandfather said I should be killed and burned, but I can't remember what I felt when he said that. I think I felt nothing, because I remember nothing. Anger might have been possible. When there's no understanding, anger is always possible. But I could not have felt any recognition, and for some reason I don't understand now, I felt no fear.

With every moment, things are getting worse for us, my grandfather said. Every minute that passes. That body hanging is like a clock.

That's true, Tom said. His voice from outside, unwelcome. The smell of steaks and onions on the griddle, popping of grease just audible beyond the drier sounds of our fire.

Maybe stay out of this, my father said.

I wish, Tom said. I do wish that. I wish I could erase when I met you. I'd lose all the years to avoid this now.

We met before we even had memory.

I'd erase it all.

You'd erase your whole life.

I would have had a different life, is all, and no matter what happened, it would have turned out better than now.

That's fear, my grandfather said. That's only fear talking, and nothing about it is true.

Please, my father said. Please just stop talking, both of you. His head bowed as if in prayer, mouth resting on his folded hands, elbows on his knees. His eyes closed. Praying to the fire, and the fire leaving shapes across him, the form of every beast from the beginning, atavistic summoning of which he was wholly unaware. We can never see these shapes in ourselves, and we can never see them in time. We can only remember them. If we go back and search, we can find all portents, every moment of our lives speaking to every other.

That body is still hanging there, my grandfather said. You don't seem to understand, either of you, that what you do or say or think doesn't matter now.

Please just don't speak again, my father said.

My grandfather rose then and stepped into the fire. His boot with all that weight above it crushing down through half-burned limbs and coals, a hive of sparks, and then he stepped out, and no part of him touched. He was not something that could burn, and the fire now was broken, the pieces of wood become individual, flames reduced to their sources and no more than a few inches high anywhere.

My grandfather continued on to the table, took his spot on the high side closest to the tree and creek. Sat down heavy and pulled his hat from his jacket pocket, an old green plaid hat with earflaps. No expression, just staring ahead into the darkness where the poacher hung and the brown of the burlap caught the light even from that diminished fire.

My father turned away now from the fire, sitting on his low stump with his hands in his pockets and looking uphill, the base of the higher ridges, the trees showing faintly against the dark. I wanted in that moment to be able to talk with him, but what would we have said?

Tom set the paper plates on the bench and filled each one with a steak and onions and slices of bread, and brought them to the table. He and I sat on the lower side, and the three of us began eating, and after some time, my father joined and ate also and we said nothing. Only sounds of chewing, the muted roar of the lantern, the water in the creek beside us, the wind above in the trees. We could have been alone, each of us, and that to me is the strangest thing now. That's something I don't understand, why there was never more connection. When I search my memories, it seems it was always this way, that every moment spent with my father or grandfather or Tom was a moment alone. And so it's hard to know why they even matter. But they were the closest people to me in my life. My mother had left before I had memory, my grandmother was dead, and these three men were all I had. They were all I knew, so at the time the distance must have felt natural, just the order of things. And it seemed inevitable that we would always be together.

We finished our food and Tom threw our paper plates into the coals where they flared and curled and died out. He washed the forks and the griddle and wiped his hands on a towel and walked into the trees to his bedroll.

My father disappeared also into the trees. And then my grandfather having to use his hands to help push up onto his feet and that unsteady walk to his mattress, the sound of the springs, rusty and old, as he settled himself in his sleeping bag.

I sat for a while longer listening to the water and the lantern, two sounds from different worlds that fit together anyway because my earliest memories included them. Anything can become familiar and seem meant to be.

I reached up and turned off the gas on the lantern. An immediate loss of light, and the water grown, the tea-bag wicks glowing red along their edges, thin lines that looked as segmented and broken as coals, and then they disappeared and all that was left was the water and darkness and then the light of stars forming against the dark outlines of treetops.

The ancient world. Sounds of water and a breeze, that mountain lit only by stars. A small band of us sleeping on the ground in these trees, waiting for morning when we could hunt. Nothing changed in all that time, in all the world.

I walked into the trees to my bedroll, laid out my sleeping bag and tucked inside, and I wish now I could have slept under hides. I wish now I could have gone all the way back, because if we can go far enough back, we cannot be held accountable.

All the air gone out of the world, and my ribs pinned down, being crushed. An enormous weight, and I woke to my grandfather sitting on me. One hand on my face, pushing my head back against the ground, his other hand high in the air, holding his knife, ready to slash my throat like the throat of any sacrificial animal.

My legs moving on their own, kicking at the ground, and my left arm, free, punching into his side, but the rest of me was pinned.

He was staring down at me, that wide expanse of face featureless and the color of bone in starlight. No recognition, only a blank look into the hollowness of the world, and that knife held high, ready.

I could have cried out, could have asked my father for help, but that would have required time and sequence, one act following another, and my grandfather above me with that knife was outside of time. That moment an eternity and also an instant, and it held every other moment between the two of us.

Waterwheels here at the creek, his thick fingers holding an impossibly tiny nail in place against a thin slat of wood, tapping with a hammer, tapping lightly, careful not to split. Placing that slat between uprights in the stream, and the wheel coming to life immediately, a pulse to its revolutions, a pause between each of the two flings from water, and that pulse a reflection of our own blood.

Those hands on the pier at the edge of the lake holding a cat-fish in moonlight. Slick dark dream created from water, from water and mud and whatever quickens in each living thing, mouth wide and gasping, rimmed by tendrils, an ugliness and beauty that would not be believed. Hands that never hesitated, that ripped that hook from deep inside the fish even if every organ inside was attached, even if the entire stomach had to be pulled out through that mouth. The tail churning side to side through air that had no thickness, nothing to push against, and the flesh in folds, loose-skinned, invented too quickly.

The lake with its own stagnant breath always close, rotting of dead carp and birds caught in the tules, rotting of algae on the rocks, baked each day in the sun and then exhaling at night. The air thick with water and rot and these mudcats rising out of that, and my grandfather made of that also. A presence that had never begun but had always been.

I waited for that knife to come down. Nothing I could do against it, my throat exposed and the rest of me helpless. My grandfather as large and unfeeling as mountains.

I can't help but think now of Abraham and Isaac, of course, and I wonder whether every story in the Bible comes from Cain. A riddle, all of it, testing a man and finding him worthy because he's willing to kill? Cain as our goodness, our faith, our murderousness as our salvation? No guidance is possible from the Bible. Only confusion.

And what does it mean that this was my grandfather, not my father? How do we read our lives when the story has veered off from what we know? A grandfather reaches further back, is more a father than the father himself. For him, the sacrifice is greater, the erasure reaching further into the future, but he also feels nothing, and so is there any sacrifice at all?

My grandfather did not come from god. I'm sure of that. He came from something older, unthinking, unfeeling. He came from something as true as rock and stars, a place of no recognition, before names. And what he offered was annihilation.

But not this night. This night the knife did not come down. My grandfather rose to his feet and air entered my lungs again and he

74

turned and walked back to his bed. A messenger with no message, sent by nothing. I lay with my heart clenching and the oxygen flooding everywhere, and I had to put my arms out not to fall off that ground.

I could smell smoke from the fire still, last smoke, and the occasional pop of a coal. I could hear water and wind rising as the blood ebbed in my temples, and I didn't know where I could hide. All places here exposed.

I waited until my pulse and breath were as near silent as they could be, and I waited until the soft snoring of the men was enough that it might include my grandfather, and then I rose in my socks, no boots, and moved slowly toward the creek. Each foot placed in the pine needles and tested, making sure no small branches or twigs might snap. Crouched and arms wide for balance, a kind of bird alighting in the shadows. The heat falling from me, the night air cold.

I passed down through camp and made it to the truck. I was not far from the dead man. His sack white in the darkness, all color leached away, and I must have swayed in place, because he seemed to be moving. A pendulum ticking away in that night, as my grandfather had said.

I stood with my hand on the driver's door and waited, listening for any sound of my grandfather, keeping an eye also on the dead man for whatever he might do, and when I could wait no longer, I opened that door and the cab light came on and my hand lunged in behind the seat to grab my rifle, cool stock and colder metal, and I pulled it free, the heft of it, and closed the door gently, only a click, and the light was off and I was standing in darkness again, blinded. I wouldn't be able to see if anything came at me. I could no longer see the dead man in his sack. I stepped away backward, quickly, crouched, the rifle held before me, and half-ran backward down that road, an ape reversed, far away from camp, and lay down in the dirt with the rifle at my shoulder, ready to skylight any man or beast that might come charging.

I had only three shells in the rifle. No extra ammunition. As quietly as possible, I levered one of the shells into the chamber, ready to fire, my finger just above the trigger. Exposed on this road, forest on every side that could be hiding anything, and my ears still useless from blood.

Lying at the very bottom of this ocean of air. Clung to that. The solidity reassuring. The haze of stars so far away they were the same as not real. No longer individual but so many billions they could create a wash of light. The origin of my grandfather the same,

76

unreachable and unimaginable, and the origin of the dead man, also, and the origin of myself. All vacuums of meaning.

★ ★ ★

Too cold in that night to sleep exposed on the road in the dirt. I shivered and rose in a landscape transformed by the moon. The road a clear white path winding upward into forest that grew more dense and dark where we camped. This is the place we had chosen, the farthest in and most hidden.

Above us, great faces of cliff and broken ridge, long pale slides of talus. Some instinct to back up close against the rock, and if there had been a cave, inside is where our camp would have been.

Standing alone in the cold, I could feel immensity, how small I was at this moment. Wearing only socks, underwear, and a T-shirt, I didn't know how I had lasted this long. Kept warm only by fear.

All was silent. Not a sound in that void. And without sound, the distances could have been anything. The rock faces impossible to gauge in size. All the world waiting, ridges in every direction as I turned. The still point, when the air had equalized and there was no breeze, and if the sun never rose, all would remain this way. Each night, it was possible to want that, to want the night to never end.

I let the hammer down carefully on the rifle so it would not fire. The metal of that rifle the coldest element, and I tried to touch only the wood, held it in both hands before me as I walked toward camp. Like the last remnant of some larger band advancing still.

I left the road as I neared, made my way up through trees to come at camp from higher ground. Large pines with cones scattered everywhere and fallen smaller branches, so that I had to test each step before allowing any weight. The walk of a blind man, each foot seeking ground and no momentum. Ready to stop at any moment.

In the forest, all vision reversed. On the road, under the bright moon, all substance was light, outlined in shadow, but here all substance came from darkness, and it felt as if the world could have been created this way. *And the earth was without form, and void; and darkness was upon the face of the deep.* This was how it began, before the light. Not absence of matter but antimatter. A void prefiguring. The first pull that shapes us.

Walking through that forest, I had to focus on the darkness, because light was insubstantial and could only mislead. The forest grew as I walked, all voids always expanding, the

78

distances seeming farther. From the road, I had seen the entire stand of pines between the rock above and road below, notched into the mountain, bordered and finite, but once I was in it, all borders fell away and new land emerged, small ridges and folds inventing themselves between me and camp and each step slower than the last.

The rifle was all I had, held close across my chest, and I was without scale, could have been any size, nothing around me fixed, and it was some time before I was above the camp, oriented by the water rushing into that sink and by pattern of moonlight on the roof above the table and on the cab of the pickup. More difficult to find the men where they slept, but I was careful, and I found the place where my grandfather had been ready to slit my throat with that knife, and I felt exposed and afraid and was shivering, looking constantly behind and to all sides, but I worked down closer through the trees until I could see the white of his mattress and his great bulk lying upon it.

I held that rifle with my thumb ready to pull back the hammer and considered hunting my own grandfather. He had come close to killing me, and it seemed he could still do so at any moment. I didn't know that I could sleep and count on waking up.

I raised my rifle to my shoulder and lined up that round peep sight with the thin vertical tip on the barrel, old metal that my grandfather himself had held when he was a boy, the rifle he had used to kill his first buck, and the dark bulk of him was softened and made smaller by this deadly alignment of fin and circle, all invention colder and smaller than we expect, its power a transgression, an opening of the heavens themselves, and this eased my fear. I pulled back the hammer with my thumb and now no one in this world had any power to stop me. Whatever would be, I would decide. And the poacher had made all possible. There was no longer anything I couldn't do.

But I lowered the hammer and then lowered the rifle. I can't say why I didn't pull the trigger then any more than I can say why I did pull it earlier. The decisions we make come from nowhere near our conscious minds. I stepped back carefully to my sleeping bag and carried it farther off into the trees, higher on that slope, found a hollow behind a fallen trunk, a place blocked from view, and lay down and tried to get warm, held my rifle close and hoped for sleep.

The darkness a great muscle tightening, filled with blood, a living thing already before god came to do his work. No first breath but an earlier animation and pulse and pressure. I lay in that darkness waiting, and I did not sleep, and the stars meant nothing but only the dark spaces between them. That was what lived and breathed and flexed. The ground beneath me swinging gently, responding to the pull, and I was caught between. A kind of trap on springs and my grandfather in his great bulk tottering somewhere in the darkness, his footfalls landing anywhere.

What can never be understood is time, why a foot falls when it does. My grandfather waiting my entire life, and something in me waiting also.

It seemed possible that I would never sleep again. My mind as clear as the cold air, fully alert, and each moment expanded and nearly infinite. That night longer than all my life before it. No scale or measure in this world can ever be held constant. We are always slipping.

But eventually I heard the pumping of the

lantern, Tom risen to cook breakfast, and the trees appeared above me, created in an instant, transformed absolutely from their shadows, made in the light, thousands of needles without true color, yellow-white instead of green, and their heavy cones and branches and the deep etchings of their trunks. All distance gone, the heavens erased. The world flattened.

I could not hear that soft roar of the lantern, a sound I loved, because the spring was too loud in the basin, but I could hear metal on metal, scraping and cutting as Tom worked, and I knew that I had passed into safety. My grandfather would not come for me now. Now the day had begun and we would all hunt together and all else that waited for us would be deferred.

I remained in my sleeping bag, in the warmth, and the breeze rose even though there was no sign yet of the sun. A prefiguring, the air itself impatient for the day. I do imagine the creation like this. A thing awaited, a restlessness.

The light of the lantern not steady but pulsing slowly enough to notice, a different kind of sun. And this camp become its own dwarf universe, separated from the darkness all around. I rose and pulled on my jeans and boots and jacket and hat, my shadow cast enormously against the slope and trees behind. Tom the largest giant of all, one swing of his arm covering my entire region in shadow and then gone again.

I rolled and tied the old sleeping bag and left it under the protection of the fallen trunk. I stepped sideways along the hill, rifle in both hands, that shell still in the chamber, ready, and came at camp from a different direction, close along the spring and its pipe and stream, the sounds of my footfalls covered.

Tom standing at the griddle backlit by the lantern. His camo baseball cap and jacket, mottled dark greens. One hand in his pocket, the other holding a spatula. He looked up and saw me.

Same as any other breakfast, he said. Same as any other hunt. Holding your rifle. But I know the difference.

Tom's face in shadow but that voice the same as I'd heard all my life.

You don't get to do something and have it be nothing. Soon as we're back, I'm going straight to the sheriff.

You're right, Tom, my father said. You should turn yourself in after shooting that man. It's the right thing to do. My father on the other side of the table, downhill, his face revealed by the lantern. He had been visiting the dead man, perhaps.

I don't believe I heard you right, Tom said. He turned away from me and the griddle, faced my father.

You heard.

No, I can't have heard you right, Tom said.

Our work here is to collect the evidence, my father said. I've put that man in a sack, and I've apprehended you, and brought you back with the evidence. Three of us as witnesses.

You'd do that.

Yes I would.

You're sure about that.

Yep. Though maybe there's no need for anyone to visit the sheriff at all. That seems better, doesn't it?

Well. Tom turned back to the griddle. First hotcakes are ready, he said. Time to grab plates.

I held my rifle down low, out of reach, and stepped just close enough to grab a plate. Tom put two pancakes on it and looked at me. I was in his shadow and could see his face now, stubbled and tired and his eyes distorted behind those glasses.

I sat at the downhill side of the table, steered clear of my father. Rifle butt between my feet and barrel coming up past my right shoulder, in close and protected. I grabbed the pot of cream of mushroom soup steaming

84

at the center of the table and poured it over my pancakes, creamy white with dark chunks, half-moons. Thick gravy, condensed without the water added.

My father sat down opposite and yet managed not to see me. I was not there. He poured the gravy over his own pancakes and cut a piece with his fork. Roar of the lantern the primary sound now, close above us.

My grandfather ambled out of the darkness to the table, and my father got up to allow him room to swivel his legs across the bench. The sound of his breath working, lungs too small for all that bulk, a heart the size of a walnut. Everything inside him shrunken away, until finally you could cut him open and find only endless fat.

A plate put before him, and he poured the gravy and began chewing even before the food hit his mouth.

My father cutting perfect double-layered triangles, as he always did. Portioning the same amount of gravy on each bite, chewing for about the same length of time, everything ordered.

And then Tom joined, stabbing his legs in beside me. His plate piled with three pancakes, taking more. He poured the white gravy and then cut in a ragged way with his fork, working toward the center of the pancakes without trimming any edges. My father always annoyed by this, glancing over as he ate. And suddenly it seemed as if this could be any other hunting trip, rising early in the morning, before the light, my father glancing over at Tom's plate and holding back from saying anything. The lantern and the spring. The wind coming up.

The dead man just playing, a joker tied himself in a sack, horsing around. I looked over my shoulder and he was there, swaying a bit in the breeze, holding back his laughter, his chin tucked into his chest, eyes closed.

I do understand that something has happened, my father said.

Hallelujah, Tom said.

But think about what the two of you have suggested. We have killing and burning my son as one suggestion, and that from his own grandfather, who apparently has lost his mind.

My grandfather said nothing in response. A jaw chewing as automatically as any cow's, eyes vacant.

And then we have the bright idea of going to the sheriff, so that we can all explain how this happened and why we brought him here and put him in a sack and on and on. We'll have lots of time in pajamas for the rest of our lives to get the stories to work out.

It's not too late, Tom said. It's still only one person committed a crime.

Not true, my grandfather said. Not true. He was staring now at the dead man, sighting him from farther off than seemed possible, and his fist on the table with the fork sticking up.

So what's your bright idea? Tom asked.

We bury him, my father said.

Bury him, Tom said. A proper Christian burial. Do we invite his mother?

It's easy, my father said. All this land, and no one here, no way to check all of it. We go out in the brush somewhere and dig down and bury him and forget about the whole thing.

As if it never happened.

Yeah.

And what happens when they come looking for him?

Let them look. We don't know anything.

And what happens when they find that blood where he was shot?

Nothing. There's no body. And we don't know anything.

We don't know anything.

Yeah.

And your son never says anything, never in his entire life. Doesn't slip and say something at school.

Yeah.

That man in the sack is not the problem, my grandfather said. You take care of that and you still have taken care of nothing.

My zombie dad suddenly the fucking philosopher.

Zombie?

Yeah, Dad, as in you're never fucking home. You're as lively as a piece of wood. And now suddenly, when there's a problem and I could use some help, you're fucking Aristotle. Hooga booga. We know not what comes from our own arses. Doing something is doing nothing. Waa waa waa.

My grandfather swung that fist with the fork faster than I had imagined possible, and now his fork was standing up in my father's forearm where his sleeve was rolled back, the tines deep in his flesh and already turning red at the edges. So sudden it seemed almost as if forks were supposed to stick up out of forearms.

Then a bellowing from my father, yanking the fork free, hints of red in the air, red even in the flattening light, and my father merged with that great bulk, a collision that reversed time, that took what had calved away and found it entire again, one mass falling backward, suspended, a fall soft and continuing, a kind of love almost, the underside of boots waving above the table now and a whump of sacks of flesh hitting earth, a snarl of sound unrecognizable to me, and nothing set in motion would ever cease. A tumbling and grunting across ground I could not see, so I stood, as Tom did, and we watched this mass work its way toward the land of miniature water-wheels and islands and channels, and these giants, at times separate, at times combined, rose and fell across that land, the water a way to mark movement, great splashes and sprays in the shadow now of the tree but carrying light anyway, a faint blue to it even when lofted, and I was standing now at the water's edge, and holding my rifle in both hands, and my father labored for me. He was crying. I could hear that. He was weeping as he pummeled my grandfather and was pummeled back, slapping sounds flat and unconnected. Tumbling into light again, farther downstream, and I saw my grandfather's mouth open, great dark hole inhaling, fueling that mass. I knew my father had no hope.

My father was weakened by a sense of right and wrong. The unjust was a weight to him, and he would return the world to a perfect order, and that can never be done. But my grandfather worked from older rules, I see now, from what shifted mountains and made light bend. He was waiting only to see what would happen, and no outcome was any less desirable than any other. I didn't know that at the time, but I had some sense of it, a fear that was wholly earned, an instinct that was unerring, an instinct my father had somehow lost.

My father lay flat on his back in the stream, face barely above water, and my grandfather lay across him looking up into darkness and used only his elbow, jabs downward and my father buckling each time, and my grandfather seemed not even interested, unwilling to make a greater effort. Only these lazy, punishing jabs, and the blank stare into nothing above.

That face, that blank stare, is what I still need to understand. How could I kill and feel nothing? Can we ever know how we have become?

This is why I keep looking to the Bible. It's almost entirely worthless, and I don't care about Jesus, but the Old Testament is a collection of stories from an earlier time, atavistic shadows that I keep wandering through, hoping for recognition.

The fight was over, my father defeated, and my grandfather rested on him, that elbow still jabbing downward now and then. The stream considering them just another island, the cold soaking into my father, and Tom and I stood at the bank and did nothing. My grandfather not a force that could be mitigated in any way. We could only wait.

And finally he rose. To his knees, pushing at my father for leverage, and then one leg up and a kind of rush and fall forward to get the other leg under him, and he kept falling forward with heavy steps across that stream and past the table and all the way to his mattress, where we heard him collapse again.

I stepped into the water, bitter cold, and pulled at my father's arm, helped him to stand and the water fall off him. He had done this for me, but there was no way to recognize that. Very little of what was important could ever be said. We had almost no language.

Dry clothes, my father said. In the truck.

So I went to the truck and found his clothing and a towel and came back to help him strip as he sat at the table. His jacket and shirt off first, and he looked pale and thin in the lantern light, jaundiced by the wicks and their yellow glow. Only hints of pink. I rubbed the towel over his back and down his arms and he sat with his chin against his chest, like the dead man, just not hanging upside down. But the two of them cold and pale and slumped and waiting, and I thought of them both as victims of my grandfather, as if the

91

dead man had met his end from my grandfather, not from me.

My father put his arm around me and I helped him stand and push off his wet jeans and baggy white underwear. Hairy and goose-bumped, and he sat back down and dried himself with the towel, slowly, and I helped him put his feet into dry wool socks and brown Carhartt pants and his boots and we forgot underwear but he said it didn't matter. I helped him stand again and he got the pants hitched up and buttoned. Then a white T-shirt and an older jacket that smelled of smoke and blood and oil. Dark green cloth that felt like oiled canvas and bore stains everywhere in great shapes like a frieze of all that had happened to us, and in a way this was true, because here were the blood and guts of unnumbered deer and fish and geese and everything else, and our history was somewhere in all that we had killed, and it was a history, certainly, without words, a history that could be told only in shapes with more direct corollaries.

The sky from black to deep blue, the dark hulks of the trees standing above us now, the lantern extinguished. Gathering our last things, my pockets filled with .30–.30 shells. The stars erasing. We would be late for this hunt, not yet in position at first light.

I waited in the bed of the pickup, one foot cold and soaked. Shivering in the cold, but the sun was coming soon and the day would be hot. The light a kind of trick, in each moment a different blue, washing out slowly. It was hard to say what blue was.

Even the sack could have been blue, and the body inside it. Hanging from that pole, still waiting. A patient dead man. And I wondered whether we would ever move him. We might not. He might just hang there forever.

Tom already waiting in the cab, and then my father walked over, stiff and slow, still cold, and finally my grandfather rose from his mattress and had somehow changed into dry clothing also, but he no longer had boots. Soft shoes instead, leather moccasins. And his head bare. The hat with earflaps soaked or gone. White hair in short tufts on either side of his head, the wide baldness between. Speckled skin, and slack, like a great white toad. Mouth too small and eyes too small, but otherwise recognizable. He climbed in, the pickup lurching and recovering, and then we drove out.

This land gone pale, all color drained. Shadow and distance only rumored, soon to be. Etchings of lines, of tree trunks vertical and fallen, of ridge and cloud and road and no distinguishing between them, only lines carved into the same flat plane. The light not a light of this world but more a temperature, a coldness through which we could see. And our movement along that road felt without orientation, as if we could be turned on our side and not know it.

And then none of that was true. The hillside became real, a great solidity extending, and the trees stood vertically and the road was cut into the earth, and the sky above was in its own separate plane and all had been made again and the previous light was only memory and not even that.

We passed beyond the area of the imaginary buck, beyond the waste of deadfall and poison oak, and I could feel it rising already along my face and neck and hands, my skin growing and itching. A distraction, always annoying, something that had to be ignored. What I was looking for was my first buck, and I would not let that be taken away.

But my father turned downward into the lower sections, thick brush and narrow low ridges, a place I would be unlikely to find a buck. This seemed intentional. The pickup winding down and then up steep fire roads like a roller coaster with the brush scratching along both sides. A constant high scree and no view anywhere, all bucks no doubt fled before us from the sound. The sky turning white and yellow. All of us straining to hold on as the truck twisted and lurched and the hood pointed into the sky and then down into ditches. A kind of punishment from my father, pointless hunt, no hunt at all.

Manzanita leering at us from both sides, deep red and peeling, taking a multitude of forms, arrays of thin branches all reaching straight upward or thick trunks twisting off sideways, leaves shaped exactly like eyes, twisting between white and green, thousands of them.

Small birds everywhere, exploding through the manzanita as we neared. Low brown swoops and landings and chittering. The baffled sound of those tiny wings against air, a textured sound surprisingly loud over the low whine of the truck. Smell of wet earth, overnight dew, our tires digging and the truck wanting to bound forward, held back constantly by that low gear.

The sun high on Goat Mountain above us, yellow on the broad rock faces, and the air seared into nothing, no color to the sky. We were still in shadow, mosquitoes wavering around me in the cold.

The bucks would not be here at this time of day. They'd be out of the brush, in the open sections, under the trees or in the glades, feeding. And my father knew that. But he kept crawling over these closed-in slopes in a place where we would see nothing. These hills shaped like a carton of eggs.

Mud in the troughs down low between hills, and the truck slid and caught and slid again and my father drove on recklessly, willing the mountain to try to stop us. He climbed again, the tires slipping, and descended into a worse trough, a place too wet for brush, mired the tires and dug out, crawled forward again, mired and sank until all four tires spat mud and water and did nothing but dig down. We were no longer moving.

My father let off the gas, and I looked over the side, the tires sunk in past the hubs. We were somewhere below bear wallow, the only area on this entire dry mountain where you could bog down in mud, and my father had driven straight for it.

I walked around the bed looking for a dry place to hop down, but the mud was everywhere. We were an island.

My father turned off the engine, opened his door and stepped out, sank to midshin. We'll need to dig out, he said.

How? I asked.

I don't know. He rocked a bit, pulling a foot free and letting it sink again. Then he looked at the sky. I looked up, too, and there was nothing. The sun coming down closer, and you could feel its heat, but we were still in shadow.

My father slapped a mosquito on his neck. Rocks, I guess, he said. Rocks or wood. Help me look for stones. Find some big ones.

My grandfather and Tom weren't moving. Apparently they weren't going to help. So I left my rifle in the bed and hopped down, my boots become surfboards, sliding sideways into the muck, gone in their own directions, and I fell backward with a great slap. My butt and back hitting the surface and then settling, sinking, the cold ooze.

My father yanked me onto my feet. Quit fucking around, he said, but there was no heat to it. He was a sleepwalker, stepping away through the mud, looking for rocks.

We climbed the hill beside us, found stones

97

and freed them and threw or rolled them toward the truck. Each stone partially buried. Some wouldn't budge, connected to too much rock below, and on these I yanked and lost some skin from my fingertips.

Like farmers tending our crop on this hillside, the sun reaching us finally. It could have been a vineyard, except the vines were dry brush, snapping and scraping against us, and the fruit emerged through the ground itself, just breaking the surface. Dark fruit with white lichen on its skin, ancient fruit, ripening long enough for the lichen to grow. Crops for a world slowed down, seasons extending for eons, winter impossibly far away. Timeless but dislodged now and thrown into the muck.

We wedged the biggest stones behind the tires, one each, tamped down as low and close as possible, my father kicking with his heel. Then the next biggest in front of the tires, tamped down also, and more stones in front of these, creating a road out. On my knees in the muck, rolling and placing the stones. Cold but the sun warming us. My father and I working together, and my grandfather and Tom seemed not to exist. It seemed like just the two of us, and I liked that.

We're getting close, I said.

Yep, he said. Closed-mouthed, allowing nothing. Hair a fringe in the light. I remember the weight of the need I felt, because I was still a child, only eleven years old. I think a child will have nothing less than ingesting a parent, swallowing them whole from the world, and anything other is a disappointment.

It was too soon that my father stepped into the cab and turned on the engine. I stood on the hillside and watched as he gently gave power to the wheels, trying to keep the tires from spinning.

Push from the back, he said out the window.

Okay, I said, and I slopped over to the tailgate and tried to push as he gave power again, though my feet only slid backward in the muck.

But the pickup lurched forward, bracing against those stones, and then he gave it more gas and tried to get momentum and the entire truck swerved off the stone path, mired to the side but with enough speed now to slide forward onto higher ground and pull itself uphill by its front tires as the back ones spun helplessly until they too found a grip and he gunned it up that hill, fishtailing and exhaust in the air.

He stopped at the very top, the body still rocking, and I waded through mud and stones and climbed that hill after him a kind of beast unrecognizable, caked entirely in mud. A bigfoot risen out of the earth and shambling along until I would dry in the sun and all movement would slow and I would be caught midstride, paused until the next rain, which might not come until winter. The rain would loosen my joints again and I would climb higher along the mountain and look for snow and a cave and come out every once in a while just to leave big footprints to make people wonder.

We like bigfoot because he's a reminder of who we were not so long ago. And if I were bigfoot, I would do my best to help the legends. I'd eat half a deer and leave its remains scattered on the road. I'd figure out some spooky noise, some hooting grunting thing that nothing else could make, some reminder that language had to be invented. I wouldn't try to explain myself. If I saw a campfire, I'd come close but not too close, and I'd snap a few sticks.

I raised my arms as I neared the truck, and tottered side to side, and moaned. More a zombie than bigfoot, but it was my first time. And it didn't matter. No one commented, if they even noticed. I pulled my great hairy bulk over the tailgate and my father knew I was there simply by the movement and drove on.

I held my rifle again and struggled to

remain standing as we twisted and climbed and fell downward into gullies. Scanning the brush for bucks, but I could rarely see more than fifty yards to either side, and no buck was going to wait that close as we thundered in.

We entered trees finally, the road still slick, and I recognized the lower entrance to bear wallow, a place I had always loved because I wanted to see a bear and had never seen one. Shaded in here, a wider gulley, very flat, the stream lazy, slowed to a stop. The earth much darker, black mud, and growth everywhere, high grasses and ferns and skunk cabbage and nettles. My father sticking carefully to the path of more solid ground that wound along one side, and even then the tires were sucking and slipping. The air cool and moist and the smell of rot.

The wallows visited recently by bear. You could see their great rounded shapes and footprints along the edges. My father stopped the truck, as he always did, so we could gaze at these signs. But this time, I was already covered in mud, so I lowered over the side and slogged through cold black ooze and standing water, home of leeches, perhaps, or even worse. I lay down in the wallows, where the bears had been, the cold soaking into me, all the caked mud loosening and blending with rot, and I did mud angels on my back.

The dead man was not the only innocent. I was a kid, and I was playing, as kids do, and the men were watching me from the truck and seemed fine with waiting, and the dead man seemed to exist in another world. We had no part in his history.

I rolled over and lumbered along through the mud like a bear cub, my belly just above the surface, hands and knees gone from view and then emerged and sunk again. The truth is, I was being cute. I was trying to be cute for my father and grandfather and Tom, and it's very strange to think of it now. This is why I can't get the story to fit together or make any sense of who I was. I had just blown a hole in someone, killed a man, and now I was acting like a bear cub. This could make sense only if killing was natural, something we were meant to do. My hands were paws and I was looking side to side, ready to snap at a butterfly or dig my snout into honey. I was in a playland entirely unlike the rest of the ranch. Giant green leaves from the skunk cabbage, curled and bright. It was possible to forget where we were.

I flopped onto my side and enjoyed the squish and ooze. I had just been a bigfoot, was a bear cub now, and I even thought of dinosaurs. Bogs and marshes and mud pits just like this were where they went to be remembered. Dying out on dry ground you could only vanish, but if you crawled into the mud, you might make it into a museum exhibit a hundred million or two hundred million years later. Truth is fairy tale. We can't really believe there were dinosaurs, because we can't imagine that span of time. We can see their bones and tell ourselves we know a brontosaurus walked and that huge neck swung through the air, but that's not the same as belief. Belief is much closer, more intimate, than knowledge. Dinosaurs happened in a different world. But killing is still with us. Killing is a past world that overlaps with ours, and if we can reach back into it, our lives are doubled.

The Bible celebrates many killings. Goliath is a bigfoot, an earlier and more beastly form of human, and this is what we most want to kill, our competitors, the Neanderthals and giants and other monstrous forms of our earlier selves. Killing the poacher, I was just like David, defending my family and our land and the law. I was on the side of god. 'This very day I will give the carcasses of the Philistine army to the birds and the wild animals, and the whole world will know that there is a god in Israel,' David says. The act of killing might even be the act that creates god.

There are times I get excited and think I did something beautiful in killing that poacher. A triumph. I wander around my small apartment like a thing possessed, pacing, and I can feel my righteousness. But then I think he was only a man, only one lousy guy back in the fall of 1978, long ago, some hunter out to kill a buck on someone else's land, insignificant. And that makes me only an ordinary killer, with no special claims.

Wallowing in that mud, playing the bear cub, I had a frightening innocence. Born into a world of butchery, a child will embrace butchery and find it normal. Or at least I did. And this was before the testosterone would kick in, before puberty. I was a monster even before I was remade into another kind of monster.

My father never did tell me to get out of that mud. He grabbed his .300 magnum from behind the seat and held its barrel pointing to the sky, pulled back the bolt partway to check that nothing was in the chamber. Then he slung it over his shoulder and began walking. My grandfather and Tom followed. We were going to hunt right here, down through brush and these hills that had no view. There was no chance we'd see a buck, and everyone knew that and began the hunt anyway.

I grabbed my rifle, followed over a lip at the edge of the wallow, and entered a different land entirely, a land dry again, a land with no hint of water. Live oak, my least favorite tree, and the shade from it spotty and low. We were traversing a wide choked hillside, not going down into the egg-crate hills, and I had never been here before. I would have lost track of the men if it hadn't been for the enormous sounds my grandfather made tearing through live oak and buckbrush. If you hadn't yet seen him, and you heard only these sounds, you'd have the most terrifying imaginings.

The sun hot and blinding, and the mud on me pulling at my skin as it dried. The spines of the live oak leaves. My jeans and jacket caked and heavy. I was thirsty, and there was no water. There was never any water. A kind of test in my family, to hike all day in the brush in the California sun and drink nothing.

I emerged in an area of gray pines. The men waiting for me, two ridges forking off below.

You can each take a ridge, my father said. We'll wait fifteen minutes and then go down through the center to flush.

My grandfather walked the ridge on the left, Tom to the right. Their rifles no longer slung but held before them, ready, and both men alert. The canyon below fell off suddenly, bits of cliff and loose rock. Tall thin darker ponderosa pines rising along steep slopes.

The canyon still in shadow. The bottom of it would see sun for no more than a few hours each day. A place that looked smaller than it was. Once we were down there, it would grow considerably. I knew that.

There's nothing I can do, my father said. You've put me in a situation where there's nothing I can do.

My father standing at the edge of an outcrop of rock, looking down. You imagine all that could happen in your life, he said. You imagine all that could happen to your son. You worry about him breaking a leg or not getting along in school, or not wanting to hunt, or maybe even what kind of man he'll turn out to be, if you ever look ahead that far. But you never see this. There's no way of seeing this, especially at eleven years old. It's just not something that happens.

Sorry, I said.

My father laughed, a bitter strange sound like strangling. Yeah, he finally said. You're sorry. Well that fixes it.

The cicadas pulsing around us, pressurizing the air. My father stepped to the side, top of a chute, and went down fast. Almost like surfing, his right hand out and touching rocks as he slid down the face. Steps that sank ten feet. Rifle slung diagonally across his back, right side tucked into the hill. White T-shirt, brown Carhartt pants and boots. He made a slalom course of that slide of rock, traversing down and then twisting in the air, planting his feet again, left hand now to the hill.

Below him, a cliff edge. This run of loose rock ended in a dead-fall I couldn't see past. Only air beyond.

I couldn't move or speak. I could only watch as he tucked in closer and planted his feet hard, hopped once more, twisting to the right. Still sliding as he stepped onto solid rock and grabbed at small scrub with his hands. His momentum should have carried him past, but he managed to cling there. And then he traversed that rock and made it to a tree that grew at a crazy angle, some twisted thin thing heading out into space, and there he rested. He leaned against it and looked up at me.

Come on, he said. It was against the rules to speak that loudly on a hunt. But our role was to flush, and maybe he just didn't care.

What I thought, standing there on that lip, was that he wanted me to die. He knew I wouldn't make it down that slide onto rock the way he had. I'd keep going over the cliff edge and then I'd be gone. He'd no longer have the problem of what to do with me.

He waved for me to come, and I almost did it. I almost stepped down into the slide. But then I just kept walking along the rim, keeping to higher ground, following the path Tom had taken, and I looked for an easier way down.

I was afraid to look at my father, but when I took a glance, I thought I saw him grin. Just one side of his mouth, but a grin, and then he was traversing again, getting away from those cliffs, crossing into a steep patch of pines that leaned in close to the slope. He disappeared into the trees, and I began my descent above them. If I fell, I'd have those trunks to reach for.

My boots sliding downward, rifle in one hand and the other clawing at plants and rock, trying to slow. Small flowers and low-growing weeds like vines but all too thin, ripping through my fingers, and I slid full body, shirt and jacket riding up, my side scratched. And still I couldn't stop. I hit pine needles, slippery, fell faster, aimed for a trunk and hit with my boots, collapsed against it.

I was breathing hard from fright. My father far below surfing through trees, and I couldn't imagine doing that. Wide spaces between trunks, plenty of room to fall through, the rocks of the creek a long ways off.

I didn't want to move. I thought about just letting my rifle go, so that I'd have both hands, but a rifle had to be taken care of always.

So I eased away from that tree and began falling again, frantically crabbing to the side to get in line with the next trunk. Dangling off the edge of the world, it felt like. A place my father would never have brought me before. All rules had changed.

I hit that next trunk and stood on it, lay back against the slope and closed my eyes, everything inside spinning, my heartbeat out of control. I couldn't rest long, though. He'd leave me behind, and I had no idea how to get out of this canyon.

I slid down to the next trunk, and the next, until I was in a chute of larger rocks, reddish and veined, and these I could climb down through carefully, the footholds solid. A river of rock in motion too slow to see. A river of flesh, dark red and marbled in white, muscle of this mountain exposed. This was not our land. I had never been here before, and I wanted to leave.

I could see my father at a wide boulder in the creek below, rifle out, elbows braced on the rock, scanning both hillsides with his scope.

The weight of the slide above me, tension of each rock holding every other rock in place, flexing under strain, and I was in a mad rush to get out from under. Running where I should not have run, one misstep and I'd have broken my leg, but I charged out of there and along the creek and stood panting behind my father.

Quiet, he said.

My breath shaking out of me, the canyon rims above seeming to pull inward, the sky receding, sucked away in a vacuum. Is this part of the ranch? I asked.

No.

My father concentrated as he scanned

those hillsides, looking for movement in the trees. The creek trickling around us. It might have cut this gorge, but it was almost nothing now, nowhere more than a foot or two deep. The rock green at my feet. Strange mountain. Large chunks of pale green with white veins running through it. A rich darker green where it was wet.

There's no way out, my father said. Not this canyon, but what you've done. There's no way out.

He shouldered his rifle and stepped down through the center of the canyon, from rock to rock at the water's edge. I followed and couldn't see what lay below us. Enormous rocks blocked our vision. Smaller stones and boulders rounded and smooth, but these great slabs of cliff had fallen and never been moved since. They'd taken trees and soil with them, some still fringed where the water couldn't reach. We never visited in winter, when all was moved and shaped. We came in early fall, at the driest time, after the long hot summer, the water gone, difficult to understand the origin or shape of anything.

My father moving fast. I struggled to keep up. The slope gentle, but rocks everywhere. We came to the largest boulder yet, blocking the entire center of the gorge, small trees growing on top, and climbed along an edge and heard a crashing and snapping, a rush of sound too much to take in, a deer ripping out of branches and leaves on the other side. My father yelled and scrambled toward the top, his rifle up already, and there was a ricochet on the rock above him and the sound of the bullet slapping into the earth beside us and a puff of dust and then we heard the tinny pop of Tom's rifle and another ricochet on the other side of the rock, winging twice this time off stone, another pop, and my father threw himself down, hiding, hands over his head as if they could stop bullets. He'd let his rifle fall, stock and barrel and scope clattering, and then the deeper boom of my grand-father's .308 and another pop of Tom's .243 and more sound of hooves on rock and my father yelling goddammit fucking stop you fuckwads pieces of shit and I was in tight against the back of that rock and breathing fast.

Goddammit, my father yelled again, and he hid against that wall and grabbed for his rifle. More booms and pops, all sounds of the buck gone now, and my father climbed up and brought his rifle to his shoulder and was swinging the barrel back and forth, side to side, searching, but that was it. No more shots, no more hooves. Only the trickle of water on all sides.

You get him? my father yelled.

An echo, and they didn't answer right away.

No, Tom finally yelled back.

Missed him, my grandfather yelled.

Nice work, my father said, but loud enough only for me to hear. He sat on a wide flat rock and inspected his rifle. I carry this for years, he said, here and in Nevada and Wyoming, in all kinds of weather, and I never get a single ding or spot of rust, and now it looks like I dragged it behind the truck.

The forward part of the stock, below the barrel, was darker wood, carved into a grip. Crushed now along the edge. The bluing of the barrel scratched, the bolt scratched, the scope dinged.

I'm so fucking angry, my father said, and then he stood and held his rifle high over his head in both hands and threw it down onto the rocks. This beautiful rifle that he loved. Crunching sound of wood and clattering and then it lay still, barrel angled upward, stock in the water.

My father breathing hard, arms hanging at his sides, looking down at his rifle. That gun is going to stay right fucking there. Don't touch it.

Then he started up that slope, taking big steps and sliding back halfway on each, pulling at rock and weed with his hands. He

113

didn't look back, and I knew he wouldn't care whether I made it out of there or not. His feet kicking into that mountain and hands ripping at everything above. This canyon the exposed flesh of the mountain, and he would punish.

I thought about picking up his rifle and slinging it over my shoulder, carrying it up to him. But he'd only be angry, even if that's what he wanted. So I didn't touch it. I followed and small rocks were flipping down the hill at me, kicked free by his boots, so I moved to the side and climbed my own path.

One hand holding my rifle and the other grabbing at dirt and rock and root. My chest against the ground, lying against the mountain as I climbed. Smell of dust and pine, the patches of needles so slick I had to keep traversing to find bare dirt and rock. Moving as fast as I could.

I didn't look down, only at the wall of dirt in front of me, and I felt that I was tilting backward, that I would simply fall off the planet and keep falling and never hit ground again. I believed that what kept me from falling was only my own will, remade in every moment.

Pox and plagues. The great flood. language turned only to babbling. Humanity erased over and over. The Bible is about our fight against god. And somehow we're more powerful, simply because of our will, because we're persistent. We refuse to be erased.

It's been a bitter fight. The great flood. Think of how many lost. Drowned like rats, no burials, no apologies, no reparations. God owes us. We have a long way to go to even the score. Imagine that wall of water coming over a hill, the sheep scattering, and you feel the cold breath of it, a thrill in that dry heat, the sudden change, and the sun is underwater, pale shafts of light reaching through the blue, and that can only be beautiful, the moments right before annihilation can never be anything less than the very best moments, held suspended. That wave breaking overhead and the sun shining through it and every pattern in the world visible in the light, revealed, and god's punishment means nothing because you can't feel that you've been bad, because you didn't start in the garden, you were only here on this hillside and then the wave came.

I had been to Sunday school since I could remember. My father's one concession to religion. He didn't go to church himself, only sent me, his only son sent in his name, ha ha.

My grandfather never spoke about religion, nor did Tom. Really they never spoke about anything except hunting and fishing.

I slithered my way up that steep canyon slope, my belly in the dirt, and I refused to be left behind. I did not pause or rest, and I kept that rifle clenched in my fist and wouldn't let go. Taste of dirt, of all that has rotted and decayed and lain dormant, all that waits and then is released.

My father disappeared over the rim and no doubt kept going, and there was no sign or sound of Tom or my grandfather, though I was exposed on this slope and my grandfather had a clear view from his ridge. He could easily have sighted in with his scope and shot me as I climbed. I would fall backward just as I imagined.

An overhang of root and dirt at the top, so I crabbed to the side and crawled up rocks that slid beneath me, and finally I made the rim. I lay for a moment on the flat and rested, out of breath and my legs burning. But then I rose, because I knew no one would wait. I'd have to be close enough behind to hear their path across that next hillside, back to the wallow.

Retracing our steps. Like ants marching along a path, atavistic reckoning that feels like discovery but is only recognition. I like that idea, because then my pulling of the trigger was the pull from some earlier generation, something only recognized, not originated. And that's how it felt. Like someone else's hand working inside mine.

That scrub hillside curved outward in a torment typical of our world, the end in sight and then not the end and then in sight again and then not the end and on and on, so that we just keep stumbling along, scraped and torn as we push through. The poison oak rising all along my skin another plague. Welts and bubbles I could feel on my face and neck and see on my wrists, the bubbles much lighter in color, almost white against the angry red, and holding some vile liquid invented where.

I wandered through live oak and scrub and sun, sweating and growing the welts, and I couldn't hear even my grandfather and his path of destruction but only my own footsteps, and so I had no way of knowing if I was on the right course, but because I'm an ant, I ended up at exactly the right spot, coming down over that lip into the wallow

117

right next to the truck. The men already in the cab, waiting, silent as stones, and I climbed aboard and we were off again. Simple as that.

We rose out of that bog into ponderosa pines where Tom had once wounded a spike, a story remembered by each of us as we passed, a story as always with a lesson but a lesson unclear. Don't shoot a buck with no fork in its horns. Illegal, and not good for continuing the population, to shoot the young ones, but something beyond that, too. Some pact made to follow code and rules even if we have no idea where they come from. In other states, it was legal to shoot does, the female deer, something we considered outrageous. Who can say what rules they follow and why? How much of what feels inviolable is only random, with no ground to it at all?

We emerged from that area of shame and the switchbacks appeared above us, bare jagged scar cut into the hillside, denuded of trees. As exposed as a quarry, white and blinding in the sun, a furnace emanating heat. And we could see there'd been a slump during the winter, part of the road caved away in the middle of the Z, but we didn't stop or even slow. My father accelerated, in fact, and we rode up on the side of that steep hill, the pickup tilting at a crazy angle and I could feel the beginning of the fall, the roll to the side, but we were going so fast the momentum carried us through and my father yanked us back onto flat road and hit the brakes in a cloud of white dust, our tires sliding. The drop-off to our right, bare slope ahead, the road kinking up to the left. My father just making that turn, the front tires grabbing and pulling us upward.

My father sped again, and this obviously was not a hunt but only a punishment. He hit a dip so fast my feet were in the air and only one hand clinging to the rear slider window of the cab, my rifle in the other hand flung skyward, and I heard one of the men hit his head on the roof, Tom probably. My grandfather too heavy and my father clinging to the wheel.

A lurching sharp turn to the right at the next switchback, and we had two tires in the air from the tilt, then grabbing again, and shot into trees, cool shade, flying along over uneven ground, bucking and sliding, pinecones and twigs popping and flung in our wake. The ride of the damned, last ride into hell, trying to outrun the devil, and I shouted in excitement, exhilarated. I glanced behind for what might follow. I kept that rifle in my hand, and my eyes teared from the wind.

My father always controlled, never one to

do this, to just stomp on the gas and go. The pure thrill and adrenaline. A gift from the dead man. A new freedom. The landscape become a kaleidoscope, rolling and exploding on all sides, without orientation. Branches whipping at us, the treetops spinning overhead, the furrows and lumps of land coming at us like waves, rise after rise and this mountainside endless, born from itself again and again and we were riding it, finally.

My father did not let up. He tore along all the way back to camp, came to a sliding stop in the pine needles just before table and stream, and our cloud of dust followed us in, washed over us and seemed a kind of blessing.

The passenger cab door opened and Tom and my grandfather were out, but my father waited a while, and I waited with him. It seemed too soon to move. The air cool in here, the reassuring sound of the spring in the basin and running lower alongside us, the breeze in the pines. Always a breeze here, even when there was a breeze nowhere else. Safe ground. And we would rest now. We'd have lunch and lie down for naps, and all would be renewed and begin again. This was the promise of camp.

My father finally opened his door and stepped out. He looked lost. His eyes searching mine and his mouth loose. His finger had been on that trigger. He had killed that man. I believe now that's how he felt, nothing less than that. The sins of the son visited upon the father. And nothing he could do to go back and change a thing.

I thought my father might say something, but he only walked away to the table to wait for Tom and the food. Reduced to habit. Sitting at the bench gazing down at the wood, not really looking at anything.

I grabbed my spare clothing from the cab, stripped off layers of caked mud until I stood bare and naked on the pine needles and kept my rifle close. The dead man in his sack directly behind me, watching always. My white skin with dark smears of mud and small island chains of red welt. The poison oak across my belly and on my privates from when I peed. Anything you touched became the property of the oak. And if you scratched, the islands grew and formed continents, entire regions of angry red and white bubbles edged by smaller darker welts, as if your skin could boil.

I pulled on a new T-shirt and underwear and jeans; found my clean pair of socks and knocked my boots together to remove most of the mud. I didn't have another jacket, so I whipped it against the bed of the pickup,

121

small shards of mud flying off.

Lunch was ready now, the men at the table with their knives. My father and grandfather on the uphill side, not looking at one another. I climbed in next to Tom and kept my rifle away.

Lighter-colored, Tom was saying. Almost gray. Silvery. Like an older buck, but I only saw forks.

Three-pointer, my grandfather said.

I didn't see that, Tom said. I only saw forks. But he was light, almost the same color as the rock. I must have looked right at him when he was standing there and not even seen him.

You'd have noticed him, my grandfather said.

No, I don't think so. I think I looked right at him and didn't see him. I think if he had just stayed still, none of us would have seen him.

In another minute, I would have been standing next to him, my father said.

Even then, Tom said. I don't think you would have seen him.

That's just stupid.

No. You never saw him, so you don't know. Think about this for a minute. He didn't jump until you were right on him, but you know he must have heard you coming, and smelled you, and he didn't move. So that means he decided to wait. He was going to hide and wait it out. He made a decision, but then he just got jumpy.

He didn't make a decision.

He made a decision.

Well. My father rubbed at his forehead with both palms, down over his eyes and cheeks.

He almost had us, Tom said. He grabbed two more pieces of bread and went for the deviled ham, smearing it across both sides, a kind of pink froth.

Not just almost, my father finally said. I don't see a buck hanging over there.

Springing around in those rocks, darting this way and that. It's only luck if you hit one in that situation.

That situation, my father said. Trapped in a narrow canyon, shooters on both ridges, crossfire from above. Be a real miracle to hit anything then.

Well, Tom said. No point in talking.

Harder to hit the buck, though, if you're way the fuck off and almost hit the people in the canyon.

You can fuck off, Tom said.

You're an eagle eye. A real sharpshooter.

Look, Tom said. That buck knew what he was doing.

No buck knows anything.

You don't know anything.

Just go back to your sandwich.

You go back to your sandwich.

We listened to the water in the basin then, a rushing sound so urgent at times you could hardly stand it. At times it seemed like it would wash us away. And it could never be shut off. There was no faucet, no way to hold it back. Only the sound and force of it increasing, magnified in that basin. Water from seams of rock deep inside the mountain. Water that fell as rain a thousand years ago and had lived in pressure ever since, released only now and what was to keep it from doubling in pressure and doubling again under the weight of all that rock.

I felt panic, my heart yanking and no room for breath. That water could rip the earth open right here beneath us. And my own blood was the same, pumping and pressurizing and no holding it back. I panicked like this all the time as a kid, my dreams all of pressure and panic, and even remembering now my breath is short. And each time, I didn't believe I would survive. I didn't know how to get through those times. My father and grandfather across from me unbearable presences. Their side of the table higher, and they could fall against me at any moment.

Time never did move again. That's what it

felt like. A moment an eternity. In memory, now, I can say we finished that lunch and got up from the table, but at the time, we were lost indefinitely and it was nothing less than that, and my father weighed a thousand pounds and my grandfather ten times that, and they were crushing me, the pressure of the water building behind them.

But the men did finish chewing their sandwiches, and I didn't eat but I couldn't, and my father was the first to rise and walk away toward his bedroll, and I could breathe again, and Tom left, also, and my grandfather had me pinned there still, his face a mountain rising in folds and crevices, white granite with dark grains and veins, and he swiveled his legs and rose and fell across that ground toward his mattress and I was released.

I walked carefully and stayed far away from that basin and from the mattress of my grandfather, and as I walked, the air began to thin, finally, the pressure easing and pulling back to where? Where does that go? The air normalizing, sound normalizing and making everything a lie, a dream, and yet only a few minutes before my heart had been made of stone.

My bedroll hidden behind deadfall, tucked in against the mountain, and I looked over my shoulder as I neared, made sure no one was watching. Then I hopped over that trunk and disappeared down low, safe in my hollow. I rolled out my sleeping bag and lay back to watch the sky above and the needles of the pines perfectly etched, each of them sharp against the blue, real and undeniable, individual, but thousands of them gathered together spiking the air. To think of how many in just the ring of trees above me and then our camp and up the hillside and across to other mountains and extending for hundreds of miles, this was a different kind of panic, not one of pressure but of vanishing outward and thinning and dissipating and this was the other panic I felt all the time back then, not of being crushed but of vanishing, pulled into vast empty space, and the two were equally terrifying and equally without source.

I closed my eyes and curled into a ball and waited, smelled the woodsmoke in the sleeping bag, soaked into it over the years, a comfort, and the smell, also, of sweat and the blood of animals of all kinds, and I was just heading toward sleep when I heard a heavy thump and knew exactly what it was. The dead man fallen.

We all waited, I think. I don't believe anyone rose immediately. And this was because the dead man was capable of anything. If he had fallen, who knew what he might do next? He had no insides, no center, so the heavy sound of that thump, the enormous weight of it, had to be his invention. His head no longer pinned against his chest, his limbs free to move, his head back laughing and he could be up and dancing any moment. He had no blood and so he followed no rules.

Like Jesus from the grave, able to claim anything afterward and who would dare not believe? The only trick that matters, cheating death, because death is the only true god.

I opened my eyes half believing I'd find his face above me, his breath that would hold no air and eyes that would fall inward and keep falling, that look on his face of wanting more. But there was only sky above, and all those needles of the pines bunched and etched and at no distance that could be known, moving closer or farther at will.

I sat up and peered over the fallen tree that protected me, and no one had risen. The camp empty, no sound of another being, sound only of that water that would never cease.

The mountain rupturing everywhere around us but making no sound. A cataclysm held back by holding my breath. And this was what death would be like, I knew. My dreams of pressure and panic were dreams of death. Forever held at the moment when all was about to rupture. The body fallen, the dead man's or our own, and the impact of that a shock driven through the center, but for one moment all still holds and it's the middle of a bright day, a time meant to be safe, only this premonition inside, these two feelings at once, of being crushed and also of being pulled into vastness.

Each of us afraid to move. But my grandfather a force of his own, heavy sounds of rocking himself upward off that mattress, and then the vision of him standing in the trees, naked from the waist up, looking toward the body, ready for whatever might be. He and the dead man brought together here for battle, because my grandfather was close enough to being death itself, formless and without feeling, a weight that might fall in any direction, and always this, unchanging, only waiting.

The dead man had every advantage,

though, in waiting. He lay on the ground in his sack and didn't move.

I couldn't remember seeing my grandfather's naked back ever before, not even once. Blotchy red and white expanse, living flesh and blood, as featureless as his face, in shifting folds and creases, armored in fat. He stepped forward toward the body and the dead man did nothing.

My father rose also and walked slowly through the trees toward the sack, his hands at his sides in fists. My father become desperate, mouth open and grim, ready for anything. And then Tom, and then me, all four of us advancing on the dead man, who coiled inside that sack, hidden, and I held my rifle ready and so did Tom. The men advancing until they were within the length of a body and then they could go no closer, and I was farther out still, walking across that unsteady earth until I stood behind them.

The dead man's boots were still hanging in chains from that meat hook. Yellow-brown work boots with their soles to the sky, hanging down perfectly in unison as if they still held him, and who could say they didn't still hold something? I was creeped out enough to believe anything. The dead man below in his sack with his face and intentions hidden and only his socks and shins visible to us. White shin meat and bone.

Well we can't leave him like that, Tom said.

No shit, my father said.

I'm not touching him, Tom said.

Another piece of fucking news, my father said.

My grandfather rolled his neck, eyes closed, rocked his head side to side, like a boxer warming up. Here, he said. Here we are.

More philosophy.

You're not up to the test, my grandfather said. You think everything has funneled down to this, but in fact everything has become possible.

What the fuck does that mean?

You're standing here at a moment when you could be anything.

Yeah, you're right. This is freedom. A real gift.

It is, actually. You just don't see it. This dead body doesn't matter.

My grandfather stepped forward then and reached down for the dead man's ankles and picked him up, the sack falling free, that white belly gone dark, a stiffness to his arms and legs.

Don't touch him, my father said.

Tom was backing away with his rifle held before him, and I was doing the same. The

130

dead man a darkened ghost, his head kinked, hands tied between his legs, looking at us from the tops of his eyes, vacant holes. My grandfather turning and swinging the body, turning like a shot putter, spinning, pulling that body in an arc and the dead man patient, holding on for the ride, his head and shoulders lifting higher above ground, levitating, and my grandfather at the center, this mound of living flesh. A hub of blood and the dead man become a putrid spoke and this wheel turned and my father backed away but not fast enough and my grandfather flung the body at my father.

The dead man lofted for a moment, an easy lift to his shoulders and his mouth open in pleasure as he sailed through warm air, the center of him still missing but that bullet hole become a second birth and this his childhood, playing on a sunny day, flung outward in pleasure but my father shrinking, caving backward, turning and his hands coming up to fend off, but the dead man collided with him, chest to chest, rolling up close to my father in an embrace, and the two of them fell back in a moment suspended forever in my mind, finally hitting ground and both shaken at impact.

My father screamed. Not something I'd ever heard from him before, but as he lay there on his back in the dirt, the rotting body on top of him, this was too much. He arched his neck and turned and threw that body off and rolled back fast away and was on his feet.

My father and grandfather with their arms curved out from their sides like wings, both ready, and I realized my rifle held low was pointing at my father, and Tom's too. I had no idea what would happen next. Anything seemed possible.

My grandfather a mountain and without age. My father would have no chance against him, but they circled closer, arms out and ready, and my father had become desperate. His mouth contorted as if he were still screaming but no sound came out. His teeth showing as if he would snap and bite at my grandfather.

There are only two choices, my grandfather said as he circled, his voice calm, no fear at all. His knees were not bent. His legs like pencils beneath that bulk, stiff and ready to snap. He could seem fragile at times, always changing shape. You can honor the man who has been killed. You can say his death meant something, in which case we have to punish your son. I'll help you put him in the sack right now, and we can do whatever we need to, beat him or burn him or shoot him and bury him, whatever we need to do to make it right and stop him. That's one choice.

My father was beyond hearing. He was ready to lunge, waiting for an opening, an opportunity, circling in the pine needles near the hooks. The dead man behind me watching also. He could rise and join at any moment.

Or we can decide the man who has been shot is nothing. He was a poacher, he was breaking the law, but he doesn't matter and the law doesn't matter. We put ourselves first. The clan. We make our own rules. So we take his body and throw it out in the brush and don't even bury it. We forget about him.

My father had circled all the way around to the dead man again, and he looked down at that body, and that's when my grandfather charged. There was no sound, no warning. Only this frightening bulk moving fast and he just ran over my father. No hard impact, only a slap against that bare skin and my father curled like a child at his father's naked breast, folded against him and then fell backward onto the dead man, a second horrifying embrace, and he rolled clear and knelt down with his palms flat on the ground in prostration. He caved forward and put his head to the ground between his palms.

My grandfather hadn't even used his arms, hadn't swung at my father, had only run over him. And he returned now for the dead man and untied both wrists. You won't take any responsibility. You won't do what you need to do, because you're weak. So you've made your decision, and this man's death means nothing.

He walked then toward the creek, dragging the body by one wrist. He passed beneath the log hung with hooks and chains and the empty pair of boots, and the dead man looked like a naughty child being dragged off to bed. His chin was stuck against his chest, frozen forever there, and so he looked penitent. He knew what he had done, and he understood being dragged away now.

My grandfather's feet in only socks, no boots or moccasins, slopping into water and sand and rock with no care or hesitation, ripping through ferns, the dead man yanked and shaken and soaked and torn. The ferns lush, deep green and unlikely, unchanged for a hundred million years, and the dead man now like how many generations before him, dragged away, and my grandfather as terrifying as any beast the world had ever seen.

Then through pines and into sunlight, the meadow, dry yellow grass and shimmers of heat, a different world entirely, my grandfather luminous, a second sun brought close. All distance collapsed, each world brought next to every other and no gate at the boundary. My grandfather's legs hidden by the high grass and so he seemed an orb that glided across that field, disconnected to the ground. The dead man leaving a wake of darker yellow, dull and not catching the light, a hollow that would not fill, and he gazed into this wake, would not lift his eyes to the sky, kept his chin pressed tight, intent.

This meadow the place of all my childhood play, close to camp, a small and nearly perfect meadow that should not have been used for this. One transit erasing all others, polluting memory. But my grandfather did not pause. Swept along unstoppable until the dead man had left his wake and disappeared into brush. We had lost them. Too far away for sound. Tom and I had not moved. We stood with our rifles and watched the far rim of that meadow. My father on the ground in prostration, and no sound from him either.

We waited and the entire mountain seemed to wait with us, all oriented toward where my grandfather had gone down over the horizon and waiting for his return, same as any sun but the night sped up and no darkness, no rest or new beginning, day after burning day without end, and he reappeared above those grasses and left no mark as he advanced upon us, an orbit that could not be changed, and nothing that had ever happened had left any effect on him.

He crossed the meadow and grew in size and crossed the threshold into pines, in shadow, extinguished, and crushed through ferns and the boundary of the stream back into our world, and he did not stop or notice us with our rifles held low and level, pointing at him, but walked right between Tom and me. If we fired now, and the bullets found some way of passing through him, we'd be shooting each other. But he did not look at either of us, the tremendous weight of him set in motion with his pencil legs unsteady and erratic until he reached his mattress, where he collapsed upon it face-first with his arms at his sides and legs flipping up behind. The sound of rusty mattress springs, coils jounced, and that was it. He did not adjust or move except to breathe, the rough rise and fall of mottled flesh and those tiny lungs buried somewhere beneath.

My father rose behind us with a low moan and Tom and I swiveled in unison with our rifles, guards at some gate that had not yet been built. But my father had no interest in us. His eyes were fixed on the far edge of the meadow, and he passed beneath the hooks and over the water and through fern and pine and into that bright grass following in the dead man's wake. A figure clothed and thinner than my grandfather, a figure with legs and a stride and a human form, having to walk across the earth and suffer. A figure on which all that had happened had left a mark.

He passed step by step across that meadow beneath the sun and grew shorter at the far end as the land curved down and then was swallowed in brush. We waited, as we had waited before, but the mountain did not wait with us. It was indifferent, my father no devil or god but only human. His return over the horizon would mean nothing.

But we waited, and my grandfather settled into sleep behind us, his breath slowed and deepened and a faint whistling all through him. A giant at rest, and it was unclear for whom we stood guard. Tom wearing a camo T-shirt, dark patches of green and brown and black, and his rifle held together with tape, ill prepared for some war not yet announced. Both of us ready to fire from the hip, not raising our rifles because it was unclear where we'd aim. As if some enormity were about to descend upon us.

But my father reappeared, a shape become smaller and bent, dragging the dead man, stepping backward across the meadow. Not following the previous wake but wandering aimless through that high grass, not bothering to look behind, only dragging. His path erratic and jointed, my father pulling in tugs, and the meadow became a larger distance to cross and it seemed too long for him to reach the pines, finally, and then drag through ferns and into the creek. The dead man's bare ankles sweeping downward a bit in the current, at play again on a sunny day, going down to the creek to cool off, a strange dead man who still had not discovered the gravity of what had happened to him.

My father pulled until the dead man lay beneath the hooks, and he dropped him with his arms flung above, relaxing, not a care in the world. He was a tricky dead man and took advantage any time we looked away.

My father loosened a rope that held a chain and hook, let them fall to the ground, and then he knelt at the man's feet as if he'd wash them, bare feet bloodless and white, not turned dark like the rest of him, but my father took that hook and impaled an ankle, hooking the Achilles tendon, just as he did to hang a buck, and the hook went in bloodless and he impaled the other ankle also and let them fall into the dirt.

Then my father rose and pulled at that rope and wrapped it around a tree to the side and pulled and sweated the line and the dead man rose again as he had before but this time with his ankles skewered the same as any buck and his arms back in praise but his chin ducked, penitent, not so wild now, understanding something of his fate, perhaps. That dark thin belly and the double birth, and as he rose, he swung and we saw that crater again, dark and unknown as any moon, and the flies gathering again, and it seemed that we had stood here before in this same moment and would stand here again and would always be raising the dead man to hang here above us.

What if Jesus had been hung this way, upside down, spinning slowly, hands partly curled, like claws, and knuckles brushing dirt? Head up unnaturally, chin against his chest, straining to see the sky past his feet. Jesus the hunter, hanging the same as any beast. The pews of every church built high against the ceiling so that we could look down into his eyes. Or perhaps we'd all lie on a bare floor, no pews at all, and gaze upward, or even hang ourselves from our feet in long rows like bats and chant as the blood filled our heads.

But his knuckles are in the dirt as he twirls, and so there can be no church at all, nothing with a floor and nothing with a roof because then he can't see the sky.

My father did not cover him. No sack to hide this Jesus, this dead man, nothing to contain him.

I stood with my rifle like a Roman guard and what could not be stopped was my attempt to read the stigmata. The human mind will always read and will never stop reading. This double birth, the entry hole of the bullet above but now hanging below where the umbilical cord has been cut, this tells us we are reborn in death. The crater behind it tells us that this mortal life was empty. This is not what these things mean at all, of course, but we can't stop our minds. I can't stop reading the dead man, even now, because I still want something, just as he will always have that look of wanting more.

My grandfather slept peacefully. Uneven breath that could halt at any moment but always kept going and no less peaceful for being uneven. I stood between him and the dead man, two forms in repose, and I didn't know which direction to face. Always turning, like that slow spin. My father and Tom gone to their bedrolls but I knew they would not sleep. They would only lie in that forest looking up toward the sky, become the congregation, following his gaze.

The trees become pillars of stone, carved in a language forgotten, and the sky our dome, the mountain behind us the apse. Floor of dirt and no ceiling that can be reached. The altar brought out through the nave to the very entrance, to the border of that stream and the sunlight and meadow beyond, the world outside this sanctuary. Simplest of altars, a hook and chain. And a great slab of marble for the priest, the mattress of my grandfather. The rest of us arrayed in fear around him.

Each mass a battle, the breaking of the body of Christ and drinking of his blood. The Christian mass more gruesome already than anything we could invent. Even the dead man hanging hooked by his ankles was tame, no drinking of his blood, no ingesting his flesh. We were not cannibals.

The repose of the dead man and my grandfather, the great calm, neither of them moving except from air, in the breeze or to breathe, that repose was why I couldn't move. I stood there with my rifle for hours expecting something to happen at each moment but there was only breeze and breath and the slow growth of the shadows, the pillars turning over the ground before me, circular movement like a dial to be read, arrangement in some pattern from the very beginning.

At times it seemed I would not stay on my feet, the world tilted so steeply. But each time it corrected, and each new position of shadow solidified and held and then slipped again. Like riding the card on a gigantic compass, caught somewhere near an edge, never in the center.

The afternoon darkened, the meadow burning at a lower pitch, all the sky still bright but deepened in color, all the white gone from the yellow and blue and replaced by gold and black, and each tree around me gained in presence, bark etched and hardened but grown.

Figures visible in the patterns of the bark, carvings on the pillars but not anything I could read. Waiting for the priest to rise again, and he rose first. Shifting sideways on his mattress, digging at an ear, deep exhale and then he rolled and sat on the edge, looked at me.

You'll need to always be like that, he said.

He was only a man, my grandfather. I could see that at moments like this, when he first woke. His mouth open in a yawn of dental nightmare, dirty fingernails scratching at his white belly, leaving pink tracks, pulling on his boots and then his brown hunting shirt and that jacket he always wore, shrinking in his clothing, his fringe of hair bent, digging a finger again into an ear. Only a man. But these moments never lasted.

He heaved forward and swung back into the mattress, springs squeaking, and heaved forward again and ended up somehow on top of his feet and legs. Paused for a moment, peered curiously around, eyes blinking, some kind of bird too fat to fly. Same thoughts as any bird, thoughts of nothing, no mind. Icy soul of anything made too long ago, bird or reptile or rock. And then he tottered off toward the outhouse.

143

Old and frail, shape-shifter. Trick of the devil. But my own blood. Walking unsteadily beneath the trees, disappearing behind the dark plywood sheets. Outrageous sounds then, as if he were a great bellows flattened. I expected to see him emerge reduced in size, but he came out the same rounded shape still, tottering back toward me and, as always, not looking anywhere. Eyes that had never seen.

You can't stay awake forever, he said.

I backed away, preferring the company of the dead man. Even with his tricks, he was safer. I retreated to that stream and ferns and hanging body, and my grandfather passed before me to the table for a second round of lunch. Made himself a sandwich with his hunting knife, licked the blade and stabbed it into the wood.

My father risen now also, no longer armed, nothing to gather, no gun and shells. Pissing next to his bedroll and then Tom rising and doing the same and the two of them wandering camp. I turned away and pissed into the stream, leaving no trace, no scent to be tracked, rifle tucked in the crook of my arm. My head turned to look over my shoulder, not taking my eyes off my grandfather.

The dead man did not smell good. We hung the meat of bucks to tenderize them, let them break down a bit for at least two days. But no buck smelled like this after only a day. The dead man making himself a nuisance, not properly gutted and no hide to remove. Bits of lung and heart and intestine, entrails, balls intact. Everything that we stripped from a buck. When I'd finished pissing, I moved farther away.

The afternoon had become hot. I could feel it at my back from the meadow, invading the cooler air. All pieces of memory that I tell myself over and over now, the most important few days of my life, days I want to remember in every smallest detail, but how did I tell them to myself then? I have no access to that mind. Grim dream in stops and starts filled with outrageous shapes.

My grandfather rose from the table and walked like a toddler to his bed to grab his rifle. Held it barrel to the sky and checked there was no shell in the chamber, or did he let the bolt slide back an inch farther and load a shell? No way to tell from twenty-five yards away. I held my rifle in both hands, ready to push down on the bale to lever a round. The rifle heavy from standing with it for hours, my shoulders stretched and hung.

I sidestepped and put the truck between us, a shield, and waited until my grandfather heaved himself into the cab, and Tom after him, and then my father came around to my side, looking at me like he had never seen me before, and then I climbed into the back.

Riding in this truck as if we shared a common destiny, as if we could be brought together. Rolling slowly out of those trees onto open dirt road, letting the earth turn beneath us. Passing the dead land of the imaginary buck, crossing into wide views and gentle slope that curved all the way up to the high ridges, rockfall and talus slopes. Afternoon still, and hot, but the time of shadows, each tree up that slope standing individually and marking itself against the ground. Every small plant and fallen branch and stone making itself known, until a hillside was more than could be seen. A texture only. The creation too much.

My father driving slowly now. This would be a hunt. Low whine of the four-wheel drive, the feel of the truck held back in gear. End of day the time when deer would come out of the brush to feed in the open and under trees.

We passed the turnoff to the switchbacks and bear wallow, continued on to the next wide ridge that sloped downward into white pines, both sugar and gray. Big Bertha coming into view, second-largest white pine in the state, a trunk ten feet thick and tapering only gradually until the very top, where it gnarled and kinked and crested in a wide flat plane of branches and needles that had always looked foreign to me, something from Africa or imagined lands, not from this place. Standing leagues above any other tree, a kind of signal, a living monument. Its bark almost pink in this light. Centuries made visible and real, a recognition of time that we could touch.

We always stopped here, always walked up to that ancient trunk and touched it with a hand, even if briefly. It had to be done, looking up into that enormity.

But my father passed without stopping, and I was still gazing back at the tree. A refusal of scale, a rupturing of normal form into this giant, an indication of what was always there lurking behind all that we believe. Any part of our world capable of this at any moment.

My father driving us farther down into the lower glades. I knew now that was where he was headed. Two wide meadows that fell hundreds of yards down a hillside, one above the other with a strip of brush between. The most open land of the ranch, rimmed by sugar pines.

The smell of sugar pines, sweeter like their name. And the enormous cones, two feet long and half a foot thick, wide petals of something not wood or flower but a substance all its own, curving outward together and darker at their tips. My father stopped in the final stand of trees before we'd enter the glades, stopped where he always had, and Tom was out to make room for my grandfather, who appeared without his rifle because he cared more for these cones than he ever had for deer.

My grandfather a collector but only of these cones. Something I never understood. I hopped down and followed at a safe distance under the trees. Cool in here, the breeze that came at the end of every day, and the pines looked silky, the pale green arranged everywhere above us in brushed arcs, a kind of sanctuary, the trees very tall, taller here than any other stand of sugar pine I'd seen.

My grandfather taking his first steps, leaning too far forward, a child in an enchanted garden. His tongue on his lower lip, mouth open and breathing hard. His hands forward, fingers open. Small hard bird's eyes hunting for seeds. He reached down for a large cone and the weight of him seemed impossibly off-center, tiny legs behind and struggling now to catch up as he lurched forward and rose up and somehow he did not fall and he was holding a cone like a golden egg, peering at it up close, giant cone that perhaps was yet another way of reaching back in time. A pinecone nearly as large as his head, and he held it as he would a child or a lover.

This is how I would like to remember him, standing with a newborn cone raised high in celebration under the soft pale sugar pines, a breeze and late-day sun reaching through, more cones everywhere at his feet. The closest I ever saw to rapture, and the only indication of something good or soft or innocent in him, the only time he might have had a soul.

Fringe of his hair haloed in the light, his fingers pink and new as if he had only now entered the world, and that tongue working gently, pulsing forward and back, his only movement, as if speech had not yet been invented. What he felt or saw was sealed away from the rest of us.

He turned the cone in his hands, and his wonder at it did not diminish. He was looking at it still as he walked toward the truck, and then he flipped it into the bed and turned away for another.

He would do this for the rest of the afternoon, until the bed would be filled with these cones. He would want to keep them all, and there would be a quarrel with my father when it came time to pack the truck again, my father sliding the boxes of gear and the cones bunching and crushing. At my grandfather's house on the lake, enormous piles of thousands of cones stacked behind the garage. A kind of nest? I never understood my grandfather, not one thing about him.

My father and Tom had wandered off to the edge of the glade, and I followed, left my grandfather to his collecting. A wall of sunlight, the end of shade and cool breeze, grasshoppers flung in arcs through hot air, butterflies and dragonflies. I had to shade my eyes from the burn.

My father lying in the dry yellow grass as if he were sunbathing, except his face was squinting in displeasure, eyes closed but no rest. Ants crawling over him, black figures on his arms and neck and boots.

The pattern of wind in the grass, sweeping up the hill in rounded blows that veered and spread and vanished again. Silver gone yellow, returned to waiting, and then silver again, pressed low against the earth. No predicting where or when but only watching and waiting, seeing and forgetting. An element we could never hold, never capture, even as we breathed it. And the land in folds and rises already, preshaped. All made silent by the trees behind us, a dislocation of sound. What we saw seemed only a dream, another place of worship, but this time the congregation was left alone, the priest become a child tottering off into his cones.

Desert the home of the Bible. We come from desert. We're meant to walk across dry ground, meant to breathe dry wind. This open glade of dry grass grown only to our shins, thin stalks with too much space between, not a place where more can grow. Hordes of us burning under the sun, water a clock and nothing more, step after step in our vast migrations, and how did we become so numerous?

Adam and Eve, then Cain and Abel, then Abel is gone, but there are enough people for Cain to build a city. We are sudden apparitions, risen out of the dust in great armies as Cain walked toward where he would found that city. Cain and the others we remember from the Old Testament are demigods. Noah lived nine hundred and thirty years. But we are more ephemeral, risen and walking, made of dust but filled with thirst. Dust that will not rest. And this is god's will, but his cruelty was to make the dust think, so that it would know its thirst as it walked.

Tom already far down that slope, a walker

the same as thousands of generations before him, dissolving into the folds of earth, visible and then gone and then visible again, patterns sweeping over him, patterns he would not see or know but would participate in nonetheless.

And I followed, as of course I would. Walking is all we know. Only the broken lie down and refuse to walk. My father with all taken away: his rifle, his will, his future. There was nothing I could do but leave him. The feel of that ground beneath my boots, ripped and changed forever, sound of it against the wind, a scab-land of spiked burrs and yellow thorns, dislocated and without source, brought here and forgotten.

Some feeling of hope at the beginning of every walk, something in the act of setting out, a pleasure. The scattering of small lizards before me, bodies without momentum, a run and instant stop then run again. Gravity with no hold at that scale.

I looked for the tallest of the grasses and pulled one from the ground, bent the end back carefully and creased it over itself and tied to form a slipknot. Squatting with my rifle close, the stock of it on the ground and barrel on my shoulder. I kept an eye on Tom where he was disappearing below and also on the edge of the glade above, where my father and grandfather were lost to their own callings.

A small loop now at the end of the grass, slipknot noose for lizards, and I stood and walked carefully, each footfall held back and erased, and I followed these tiny remnants of time, plated backs and scaled necks, holes only for ears and expressionless mouth, eyes direct apprehenders of the world, no mediation, no thought. The first hunters and no desire to hunt but only shadows of movement and instinct to devour. If I held still, I became the same as any rock, unrecognized. All forgotten instantly, each moment new, the world as it is. On moving, I became something again. And so I became rock then movement then rock then movement then rock again across that desert until the yellow stalk I held outstretched with its loop hovered just above a fat lizard with blue along the sides of its neck.

I was very still, and the grass in my hand trembled only slightly, moving less than the stalks around us that leaned over and shook and went upright again. Sound of that to a lizard. Head jointed, twitched to one side, cocked upward. Body a sack of thick skin, slumped.

I lowered the noose very slowly, and the lizard cocked its head the other way, gauging what? I lowered until the edge of the loop came down past his chin, and then I yanked back and up and the lizard dangled midair in a panic that reached back to everything that had ever crawled. Legs and tail thrashing at air, body kinking, all soundless. The wind in the grasses and trees all that I could hear. I held him up close, looked into his eyes, and still no recognition. Tail a snake in a wave pattern, as responsive as water in wind, just as conscious. Yellow collar, blue throat, warm air, all equivalent.

I lowered him to the ground and he charged at the collar. I let go. A lizard now with a stalk trailing, and perhaps it would trail always.

Every field populated. Humans not sovereign. The lizard a predator, a giant, but not enough of him to cover this ground. All has been taken over by insects. Hundreds or thousands within reach no matter where we stand. I went down on my hands and knees, the rifle in dirt and bare grass, and watched the infestation. Ants black or black and red, polished and untouched and their legs not quite reaching ground, suspended just enough to leave no track. Stink bugs a dull gray and folded, bright orange along their edges. Grasshoppers nearly invisible against the light brown clumps of dirt, waiting until the very last moment to jump. The activity of the world mostly invisible to us.

I rose and walked again, the hot air and late sun a pleasure, even the lizards and insects a pleasure, something about being that age, something I have trouble recovering now. I look at a field now and see nothing but time.

But when I was eleven, time was unlimited and unknown, life a thing that stretched infinitely, and I walked through grass without being able to feel my ankles or knees or back, nothing yet failed, joints a rumor only, muscle and bone not yet separating. I felt no guilt at all, no remorse, and no worry as I know it now, only impatience, only movement, and this slope caved and rose and the wind swept past and I could see across to other mountains and feel the mountain rise behind me.

I was looking for bucks again, along every edge. Approaching the line of brush and trees that divided the two glades, I slowed and crouched and kept my rifle low. The shadows stretching toward me, a thin ruff of cover. I ducked beneath branches of small gray pines and found Tom sitting against a trunk, hidden in shadow.

No sign of a buck, he whispered.

I sat against a trunk ten feet away. Our rifles across our thighs. A few more trees in front of us and then the bright yellow of the enormous glade below, large enough to be its own region. A ridge in the center with rock outcrops. A fold to the left that fell down into a large stand of sugar pines. Wide arcs of open field to either side, and a line of brush high on the right, a fire road hidden behind it.

Breezy here, cooler in the shade, cicadas pulsing. Large dragonflies cruising the margins. A few small white butterflies in their jagged flights just above the tips of the dry grasses.

I was there the day you were born, Tom said. There was no sign.

Sign of what?

Nothing to warn us. If anything, you seemed like nothing. I had a beer, I got bored, and I left.

What was my mother like?

Ask your dad.

He never says.

Well.

The lower glade a great burning disk, and we rode an edge of it, tilting higher. The heat of it.

It's not just that you've done one thing, Tom said.

What's that?

The problem is that you're never going to

follow any rule, ever.

What does that mean?

It means nothing. That's the problem. There's nothing left to hold anything together.

I didn't understand what Tom was saying. I do understand now. And I wish I could talk with him now. He was my best chance. My father and grandfather too distorted. But at the time, I said nothing. I only looked at him, this familiar face, eyes floating somewhere behind his glasses, this face like a boy's.

I would help, he said. You know that. If there were anything I could do for your family, I would help.

Thank you.

Well enjoy your last freedom. You'll be sitting here like this, but the tree trunks will be bars and the wind will smell like piss and shit and sweat and puke and your butt will be on concrete. You won't be holding a rifle. No one could have seen what you are, but they'll all find out when we get back. And from then on, every time anyone looks at you, you'll see what they think of you.

I looked out at that burning plain and the rock outcrops in the center, heaved up and broken. Scattered remnants fallen to both sides, broken long enough ago they were covered in lichen. But of course that's how I see it now. At the time, I saw the glade, the outcrop of rock, and I thought nothing of it, had no sense of nostalgia or time or ruin that could make broken rock the scattered remnants, had no more thought than any lizard during moments like this that might have held a key. All wasted on my younger self, and I wish I could remember exactly what Tom said, because there might have been something more, something that would help now, but what I remember most is what he said next.

You'll rot for thirty years. And when you get out, I'll be waiting. You'll feel it before you hear it, the rifle slug in your back. Just remember, when you get out, that's what's coming.

I remember that clearly because of the shock of it, because it was not like Tom, didn't fit with any other memory of him.

Tom walked into the glade, into the heat and sun and grasses, and angled off to the left, downhill. Camouflaged T-shirt and jeans, crouched, moving carefully, returning to the hunt.

And so I hunted too. What I was born for. Emerged in the light and followed the edge of brush uphill, remained close and hidden against it, my right arm scraped at by spines and thorns. The lower glade an arena, and the two of us circling along its edges in opposite directions.

Tom working his way toward that stand of sugar pines at the bottom, but I could see nothing there except shade and more of the cones that appeared giant even from a distance. Tom become smaller and nearly invisible against the dark brush, known only by his movement. What we expected to find was unclear. We could already see the entire glade, and there was plenty of space under those trees, no place for a buck to hide. We were circling a great emptiness.

I was close to the fire road hidden somewhere behind this brush, and then I was pushing through, leaving the glade and Tom, trying to become thin as the branches clung. Stepping sideways, rifle out front in my left hand. The scratches along my arm a pleasure, a relief from the itching welts and boils of poison oak, and then an ache. I could feel it spreading and growing in this heat, taking over more and more of my skin. Welling along my belly and sides, scraped at also as my T-shirt rode up, a pleasure and pain surging. Dry, everything dry, and I hadn't had water in hours. Dizzy and the top of my head wavering. And I wondered if I was off course and the fire road not here at all, just wading into dry brush that would never end.

159

The brush became only thicker and more difficult, as it always does. And I thought of rattlesnakes, of course, beginning to panic. Trapped and held in place, trying to ram myself through, head yanking around to look in every direction at once, skin on fire from the oak, the sun burning down and no air to breathe. Where my feet stepped, I couldn't see.

Duration. What nature offers us is duration, the promise that when we panic and are trapped and want to be anywhere else, that moment will extend and continue and grow and become only worse. This world invented for reasons that didn't take us into account, but we forget that and so we underestimate.

I panicked and reversed direction, as we do. Tried to go back the way I had come, dragging the rifle behind me now. But what I had passed through had become more impassable, each branch and thorn accelerated in its growth, and before long I had veered off and was on no path and no longer sure of direction.

No compass in fear. The world spins and tilts and cannot be held constant. Trapped and also lost, and snakes everywhere. Our first fear, the serpent, with us from the beginning, the source of dread, the external form of what we feel writhing in our hearts.

I reversed direction again, lunging for the fire road, veering and lost in new brush, pushing through with my rifle. Scratched and raw and consumed in heat and fright until my hand with the rifle hit open air and I pumped my legs and pushed through and was born onto the fire road, released.

I felt the buck before I saw him, felt the recognition and charging of every muscle, and I was already pushing down on the bale, levering a shell. He was sideways to me, no more than a hundred feet away up the road, rear haunches compressing and head going low for the spring, the sun behind me and every hair on his gray-brown hide visible in this late light. A big three-pointer lit up in the sun, just as I had imagined the day before, become real now, thick horns undeniable, large black eyes and a soul.

His eyes looking at me for only an instant then turning and he threw himself forward into air and brush, thin lower legs and hooves angled back, rippling of muscle, a beautiful symmetry and power, and my rifle was already up at my shoulder and I aimed without the sight, aimed only by feel and pulled the trigger without any decision as he dissolved into brush and only the back half of him remained and the rifle kicked against me, an explosion and smell of sulfur and some great shock to the rear half of him like the hand of god, some terrible blow that swept his haunches sideways and pulled him back from the brush and flattened muscle and shattered bone. The back half of him thrown down into the dirt, and the rest of him came after, screaming. No different from a human voice. Screaming and his head back, voice raised to the heavens in pain and confusion and rage. High-pitched, no beast, no bellowing, but human and frightened.

Dragging himself toward me, front legs digging in, head ducking and chest raising as if he would stand, but each time the rest of him failed to respond. The back half of him made of lead, only a weight to pull across the earth. He screamed again, and he did not understand what had happened. He wanted to turn around but couldn't, head yanking to the side, and every effort brought him only closer to me.

Did Cain hesitate? In the field with his brother, wearing the hides of Abel's sheep scraped bare, and Cain a tiller of the ground, his crops found wanting by god. Rage as they walk through the furrows he's planted, and he's carrying a stone, and without any thought at all he steps behind Abel and smashes that stone against his brother's skull. This part is easy.

But Abel is still alive. One blow isn't enough. Abel's mouth open in pain, eyes closed and blood in his hair from where the stone has crushed bone and torn flesh. He's on his side in the loose dirt, hands and feet numbed but clutching at the earth anyway, attempting to crawl away in the oldest of instincts. And Cain standing there with the stone in his hand.

The rage in him is gone. Flimsiest of emotions, a cover and never itself, a betrayal. Cain feels tricked. But it's too late now to go back. And so he has to kneel down over his brother and see his brother's face as he brings the stone down again, and this time Cain is shielded by nothing, this time he knows who

163

he is. And here is where he may hesitate. It may be a long time before he brings that stone down, and it's in this moment we can know Cain. The momentum of his life, everything out of control, everything misunderstood and recognized too late, that's how we are descended from Cain. All that was instinctual suddenly bearing consequence, our animal nature betrayed by consciousness.

The Bible has nothing to do with god. The Bible is an account of our waking up, an atavistically dreamed recovery of how we first learned shame in the garden and first considered ourselves different from animals, and Cain was the first to discover that part of us will never wake up. Part of us will act according to instinct, and that will never change. And one of our first instincts is to kill. The Ten Commandments is a list of our instincts that will never leave us.

I stepped away as the buck crawled toward me. Front legs pulling at the ground, trying to turn but only coming closer, dragging down that fire road. Heavy breath in close, eyes rolling, the smell of him, and then that scream again, eyes lidded and head up, high-pitched wail of every pain that had ever been, limitless and unendurable. Discovery that half of him no longer responded, half of him lost, maimed, and never to be made

164

whole again. Unable to flee, crawling closer to the end.

Smell of hide and sweat and blood and fear. Blood caked with dust, red and then brown, hind legs tangled and dragging. The fire road narrow, thick brush leaning in, and no escape for either of us to either side.

The buck coming closer. Fueled by panic, hooves working, those antlers white-tipped and ready to gore. I needed to step backward faster, but I felt frozen. The brush closing in, this long alley narrowing.

His forehead raised up in a ridge, muscle and vein beneath his hide, jaw clacking. Paired hooves, twin wedges of bone striking at the ground and pulling. And he tried again to rise, long neck ducking and charging and that wide chest coming free of the ground, up on his forelegs and then falling again.

Great exhales, snorts into the dust, and he was mired in place. I could tell some part of him wanted to stop, just lie down and wait to die. Some part of him knew it was over. I had felt nothing in killing the poacher, but this was different. I could see what the buck felt, the catastrophe, all lost, no hope of recovery, the end of a life. I felt that end. We hunt the largest animals because they are the closest to being us.

But he pulled again with his forelegs and

raised his head and crawled toward me, dragged himself closer, and I stumbled backward and fell, sprawled out on the ground before him, and I was crabbing backward pushing with my hands and heels at the dirt and he was close now, moving faster, crawling over my rifle, which disappeared beneath him, and his head yanking down as he advanced, swinging those horns.

This is the way I still see him, gray-brown hide in that late sun, each individual hair, all created in unison, a landscape of muscle and bone and blood beneath the surface, leaving ripples. The sound of his breath, hot heavy blasts, and the heat and smell bearing down on me, and I had forgotten his pain, forgotten he was maimed, forgotten what was happening here, pushing at the dirt trying to escape, and then he screamed again, a scream broken by intakes of breath, and he shook his head back and forth as if he could free himself from the pain, wring it from his body, and this was unbearable. I rolled to the side and got to my feet and ran down that fire road, ran hard and did not look back until I was a hundred yards away and safe and he was no longer near.

But of course I was still on this road, and so was he, and I no longer had my rifle. The shadows long, half the road gone, and the breeze increasing, last heat of the day. The two of us on this slope.

Nothing to do but walk toward him again, and what would happen when we met I didn't know. Then Tom appeared higher on the road, and he was armed and I was not and no one else was there to witness, and I wondered whether that slug might come now, all things sped along in our lives, impatient.

But Tom only stood watching. No celebration for killing my first buck, no hoots or whoops. I hesitated, afraid of both Tom and the buck. The buck still crawling down toward me, his head dipping and rising. This fire road overgrown on both sides and beginning to grow in the middle, brush rising between the tracks. The buck snagging on this, held back, and I thought at first his legs were tangled but as I came closer I saw my rifle trapped beneath him, caught up in his dead legs and sticking out to the side to snag.

My rifle covered in blood and dirt, and the buck kept pulling but the snag turned him in a slow circle in the middle of the road. No longer headed downhill but crawling to the side, head butting into the brush and his back to me. Haunches flattened, unresponsive.

I walked close and didn't know what to do. The buck was trapped now. His hind legs and the rifle tangled in brush in the middle of the road and his antlers caught in brush at the side. His front legs still pulling at the ground but only digging now, raising dust. Blowing with the effort, heaving and sucking at the air.

Tom only fifty feet away, the buck between us.

How do I get my rifle back? I asked.

Not my problem.

Well have you ever seen this before?

Nope. Everything with you is something new. You're the devil's own private piece of work.

Just shoot him for me.

Nope. I'm not going to do that. I'm just going to watch.

The buck had stopped digging. He was swaying in place, the front part of him moving forward as if he'd rise, then falling back, then moving forward again. Smell of fear, an actual smell, something rancid and maddening, something that could make you want to grab his neck in your teeth and just bite through.

The rifle buried beneath him and only the stock and bale visible on the other side, caught in a clump of brush.

I pushed at his rump with my boot, felt the hide slide over muscle. Dead flesh but he must have felt some movement, because he thrashed at the brush, freed his horns.

I knelt down and reached over him to grab for the bale of the rifle. Panic. He yanked his head and the horns came close and I fell back. Antlers with wide forks on top, dark brown and ridged. His eye rolling in fear and rage. He couldn't reach, couldn't fold himself far enough. His hooves slipping in the dirt, trying to lever his head back farther.

I could see the bullet hole in the side of his thigh, a small, loose hole in thick muscle and hide, and a bigger hole in his lower back where the bullet had exited, tearing through spine and then muscle above. White bone, blood, and darker meat.

Smell of a deer not like anything else, a stink from glands near the Achilles tendons, a scent for marking territory. Musky and overpowering.

I leaned in low and close and grabbed on to the rifle, but it wouldn't budge. The buck heavy. He knocked me in the head with his horns, but only a sideswipe.

Hollow. That's how his horns felt. No substance to them at all. Things imagined and sprung from air. Nothing to fear from an animal, made only of what I could tear through with my bare hands. So I came in low again and grabbed the bale of the rifle and tried to dislodge.

The buck heaving and striking at the earth

and snorting, and all was held in place, immovable. So I pulled at his leg instead, but when I let go, it sprang back. Dead, unfeeling, unresponding, all nerves cut, but still held together by muscles like springs. I tried grabbing both legs and pulling, heavy, and the buck screamed again, tongue arched in pain, and it was too much.

I fell back in the dirt and just lay there. The sky a deep blue, rounded dome above us, a vacuum into which all was taken away, every sound and pain and thought. I was breathing hard, panicked. The two of us lying here on this ground.

You need to finish that animal. It was my father's voice.

I looked up and saw him standing beside Tom.

I can't get my rifle.

You need to finish that animal now.

The buck's head swaying back and forth and a low moaning coming from him, a sound of fear, two men standing just uphill and me on the ground behind. A proximity impossible in his world, the same as if we found ourselves before our gods, all that we imagine materialized in an instant, all made real. And no way to run, legs frozen. Neck low and flat, hiding from the sky.

I crawled closer to his back, where half a

foot of the rifle's barrel stuck out, and I tried to grab that barrel, but it was pressed against the earth by all his weight and wasn't moving.

So I tried to roll him. I grabbed his hooves on the uphill side and swung them in an arc high to twist downhill, but the weight of him was enormous and unlikely and his legs so stiff I couldn't get them to point even straight up. I had them over my shoulder and was pushing hard, like some beast into the yoke for a plow, but he was pushing his front hooves downhill, twisting the opposite way, refusing to be turned. As if he were trying to run away from the men, facing down that fire road.

I dropped his legs and just stood there breathing hard and he faced again uphill, tried to pull himself toward my father and Tom. Nothing he did made any sense.

Shoot him, my father said.

I can't, I said. I can't get my rifle.

I'm talking to Tom. Shoot him, Tom.

Nope.

Fucking shoot him right now.

Nope. This is your own clusterfuck. I'm no part of this.

My father grabbed at Tom's rifle then, his hand catching the barrel, but Tom held on. The two of them up close, almost like dancing, all four hands on the rifle that stood like a needle pointing straight into the

171

heavens. Slow turns of the dance in yanks, a needle controlled by some random magnet below but always remaining upright. A needle that would shift over the surface of the earth searching for something, for some element we knew was missing, something not yet discovered but its presence felt.

My father with his eyes closed, a diviner of this footwork, mouth open in what was more disbelief than determination, hanging on, but Tom had his eyes open and he kicked my father in the knee.

The needle tilting as my father caved to the side, no longer pointing, all divination lost, and Tom kicked the same knee again and my father let go of the rifle and went down, landed on his side in the dust and Tom backing away.

Get off me, bitch, Tom said.

You don't know, my father said. You don't know anything.

I know all I need to know.

You don't know what this is like.

Yeah, I feel real sorry for you. You've been such a good person and done all the right things, how could any of this have happened?

Well I have done the right things. I've been a good father.

And we have the proof right here.

My father on the ground not far from the

buck, and he rose up to kick the buck's horns. A swinging kick from the side, and the buck's head jolted and he lowered his antlers and tried to face my father but my father kicked again from the side.

The buck braced on his forelegs, a wide stance in the dust, and raised up his chest, swung those horns on his thick neck. But my father was quick, swung his boot from the other side now and clocked the buck again.

What the fuck are you doing? Tom asked.

If you won't give me your rifle, this is all that's left.

That's just stupid. You can't kick a buck to death.

Watch me.

My father crouched like a wrestler and stood close to the buck with his hands ready and grabbed those antlers as they swung, grabbed both big forks and kicked down through the center, kicked his heel into the buck's nose.

A great roar from the buck, as if he were some other kind of beast, mythic and brutal, half giant, and he yanked his horns upward and my father was thrown back again into the dust.

Footfalls of other giants coming to help, as if the buck had called his kind, a crashing through brush, a summoning, snapping of branches, and my grandfather emerged, holding his rifle high. A beast himself.

Why is that buck still alive? he asked.

It's not, my father said. It's about to die. Stay out of this. And he rose to his feet again and held his knife this time.

That buck belongs to your son. He has to kill it.

Suddenly there are rules?

There have always been rules.

God you're full of shit. I don't know how I didn't know this about you before.

He's going to kill that buck.

And how's he going to do that? His rifle is trapped under the buck.

How did that happen?

How the fuck should I know? My father turned back to the buck and crouched with his knife and grabbed at the horns with his other hand.

The deafening boom of my grandfather's .308, shot into the ground. Ears gone blank and smell of sulfur, evocation of hell at our feet, and the buck writhing and screaming high-pitched in horror.

My father shrank to the side against the brush, just instinct, and I was up against brush too, and Tom also. All of us wanting cover.

He has to kill it, my grandfather said. It's his to kill. That can't be changed.

Obligation. What's required of us by god. The order of things. We sow what we can, but god found Cain's offerings inadequate. And nothing more that Cain could do. What if it's not possible to please god? No offering sufficient, but an offering required nonetheless.

That buck was what my family required, and yet it wasn't sufficient. No celebration. But my grandfather made sure it would be my kill.

I circled the buck from lower ground. Head turning, hooves digging, trying to face me. Tiring, bleeding out, coming closer to some dull recognition.

On hand and knee I crawled across that dirt, shoulders ducked close to the ground, and when I was so close my face was almost touching the hide of his back, his head and antlers yanking, trying to see me, I leaped from all fours and wrapped my arms around his neck.

Thrashing, risen up from the earth, that neck still alive. Every beast made for man, put here for him, but of course that's a lie. The buck fought for his own dominion, roared and shook his horns and yanked his neck and tried to throw me off. What I knew was that he wanted to live. Something I could never have felt for the dead man, the pull of a trigger too easy, a trigger something that makes us forget what killing means. But in my hands I could feel the pulse of the buck's neck, the panic in him, the terrifying loss, the impossibility that anything could ever be just, the tragedy of our own death, incomprehensible, and the will in us to disbelieve. In killing, I was taking everything. And what I destroyed could never be remade. I knew that and reached for my knife.

My left shoulder slammed against the ground over and over, and I was being shaken loose, gripping with that arm, and I would have let go if not for my grandfather watching. I had lost the desire to kill. I would have reversed time and not fired my rifle, let the buck leap into the brush and escape. I felt remorse, though I had no word for that at the time or even any possibility of understanding the concept. We were put here to kill. That was immutable. It was family law and the law of the world. And I reached for my knife because my grandfather was there to enforce. But who I was had changed. From that moment on, every kill would be bitter to me. Every kill would be something forced, something I did not want.

And that's what would make me human. To kill out of obligation, to kill even when I did not want to.

I pulled my knife across the buck's throat, and it did not cut easily. I had to saw back and forth as the buck screamed like any human and flailed and thrashed and did not want to die. And even when no sound would come out, when blood was everywhere and the buck's throat cut and filled, I knew he was still trying to scream, and I'm glad I could not see his mouth or eyes and could see only the stiff hairs of his hide as he struggled and fell and shook against the ground.

Bathed in blood. The buck still jerking. And I just kept sawing, kept cutting deeper and deeper until I could feel the blade against bone, against spine, and then I let go of the knife and just held on until the buck moved no more.

No animal should be treated like that, Tom said.

Every animal is treated like that, my grandfather said. He still had his rifle to his shoulder, ready, barrel pointed at the ground just uphill from me and the buck, as if he might shoot again at any moment.

We've never treated a buck like that, my father said. Never in our lives. Never in all the times we've hunted here.

We've done the same thing every time.

No we haven't.

You think somehow you can be safe. You think you can be untouched. You think it's possible to be moral.

More philosophy.

My grandfather smiled then. Smiled at my father. Different than I had ever seen him do before. And then he turned, still smiling, and pointed his rifle at me. Time to gut that buck, he said.

I thought he was going to pull the trigger. I froze, just instinct, and my father and Tom froze also, and waited. Whatever happened, they were not going to interfere, apparently.

But nothing happened. My grandfather only waited, his rifle pointed at me, and I unlocked from the buck, pulled my arm free from under his neck. I hadn't realized one of my legs was around him, heel digging into his stomach as if into a stirrup. I freed myself and knelt in the dirt.

The buck's eye still open, and he did not look dead. Only stunned, held in suspension somehow, but his face still the face of something alive, still taking in the world.

I scooted around to the front of him, my back now to the men. I could feel my grandfather's rifle on me still. I turned my knife blade up and snagged the tip in the center of

178

the buck's belly, white hide, and I was careful to snag only the surface. Any deeper and I'd cut into the pale green stomach sack and release bile.

I was facing directly into the sunset, downslope on this fire road, and the sun was lying fat on the horizon and burning hot in my face and the breeze had died. I don't know where it could have gone. I tugged lightly at the knife and the skin broke and the white hairs bloodless. The knife low and parallel to the cut, my fist lower against that belly, keeping everything at the surface, and as the hide parted a few inches the guts swelled into the gap, fragile membranes, slick and pooling in the light but I was partially blinded by that sun and worried I wouldn't see the tip catching a membrane, so I slipped my left hand in below the knife, fingers caressing the entrails and riding just beneath muscle, the blade skimming through above.

Ritual. What it does is make the horrifying normal. I was settling in to this gutting already, finding it easy, no longer feeling anything at all for the buck, for the life I had taken. The killing of a few minutes ago already far in the past, shielded. And the men calmed also. No more speaking, only standing in place and watching what they had watched a hundred times before and had themselves performed from the first day they were men.

A ripping sound through muscle and hide, tearing of all that had been woven together, the blade sharp and able to slide along that surface. An opening of all that had been concealed, the inner workings in each of us, a man not so different from a buck. Opening until the sternum, rib cage, brisket, end of the cut.

I wiped my knife on his hide and resheathed it, and then I opened that belly, both hands pulling the muscle away, dark cavern of heat and steam and walls of blood and bone, and it should have spilled out toward me, but the buck's belly was facing uphill and this would not work.

I grabbed his hind legs and stood with one foot on the stock of my rifle, to keep it pinned. I swung those legs straight into the sky and then heaved against them and this time the buck could not twist against me. This time I rolled him, hams first and gut and chest, then stepping forward to grab his forelegs and rotating those, too, and pulling at his antlers to flop his head.

I knelt, my back to the sun, the buck and men before me, and as I opened that cavern again all was made iridescent in the last light. The stomach sack the largest orb, green-gray with hints of pearl, the liver a deep red in loaves shaped and set here somehow and impossible. The intestine a yellowish and lumpy tubing. The diaphragm shimmering, thinnest of walls. All sliding toward me, spilling out against my knees. The breath of it.

I used my knife to cut the diaphragm in a large arc, thin sheen falling away to reveal lung and heart and rib, cut the esophagus, and felt in the intestines for the colon, stiff tube, raised this into the light and cut through then ran my hands along it to discharge the dark pellets until all was flat and smooth and empty.

I cut through the large vein and artery that fed the liver, resheathed my knife and reached in close and scooped everything toward me with both arms, gentle shifting of dough, my fingers easing apart membranes, but what was remarkable was how little was attached. These guts living separate from the rest of the body, in their own world. My face against his hide, his scent and sweat mixing with these other vapors, and my arms pulled from this other void unrelated to him.

My hands sliding along the walls, searching, and finally all was smooth and I scooted my knees back and pulled everything onto the dirt.

Save the liver, my grandfather said. Don't let that liver touch ground.

I made sure those dark red loaves floated

181

on top of the mass that had become a creature entire, its own being. Something dredged
up from the ocean, slick and shielded by no
more than membranes, brought somehow to
this dry slope of burr and thorn. Intestines
like tentacles.

I would leave it here, and it would dry and
pucker at the surface and deflate and be torn
apart and eaten by coyotes and ants and
everything else, but I knew that first I would
have to eat part of the liver. I would have the
first bite. I looked up and could see all three
men waiting. Turned gold-red by the sunset,
their faces no longer white, the landscape
bled into them. My grandfather with his rifle
held low now in one hand, no longer at his
shoulder. Face creased and unreadable, gone,
soulless, only waiting.

I cut away a hunk with my knife, a hunk
the size of my fist. It had to be enough to fill
a hand. How did I know that rule, and was it
even a rule? Or was it a discovery repeated in
each of us, inevitable?

I knelt before that buck, before the men,
and lifted raw liver to my mouth. Still hot as I
bit down through, and no resistance, only hot
mush that tasted of blood. I could feel myself
retching but held it back and chewed and
swallowed and bit again and thought of the
dead man, thought of eating his liver and

could feel the bile rising, my chest and throat convulsing, but I held it in and swallowed again and could taste the inside of every man and beast, could taste that we are made of the same things forgotten and ancient beyond reckoning from when the first creatures crawled from the soup. Taste of seawater and afterbirth in my mouth, reminder of where we came from. And why hadn't I done this when I killed the poacher? It was the same. Everything was the same, and I should have tasted his liver and then his heart.

I mashed what was left of the liver into my mouth and made myself finish it. Poison catcher. A taste I wasn't sure would ever leave.

The sun gone down, in shadow now but still reddish, the men waiting. I had the heart still to eat.

Torn diaphragm sagging in remnants, lungs frothy looking, orange tinge to the red. As if our breath were foam, a reminder again of the sea, of our origins. And the heart hanging in place rigid and marbled in white, a thousand miniature designs reaching upward across its surface, every thread of muscle and blood and fat.

I grabbed this heart in one hand, tough and rubbery, same size and shape as a human heart, no different. My other hand holding the knife, reaching upward inside to find the large arteries and veins and cut through, vines in a forest enclosed. Severing all, and more blood, endless blood, running out now hot over my fingers. I pulled the heart free, held it in the open air and turned it over to drain onto the dirt, blood heavy and thick and pooling in the dust.

Domination. To hold a heart in the air still warm and take a bite from it. Proof that all was created for us, for our use. An assertion repeated and echoing through time.

I sank my teeth into the wall of that heart and it was so slick and rubbery I had to push it hard against my face. My teeth not made for this, not sharp enough, so I shook my head as I bit, tore at the muscle. My knife dropped and the heart held in both hands, and I was made a beast again, eyes closed and jaw working and the taste of blood and flesh in my mouth.

Now you're a man, my grandfather said.

Now you're a man, my father said.

I let that heart drop and roll away and I chewed until I could swallow, and I felt my life had begun. Eleven years old and now a man, blood all down the front of me. The sun fallen and the shadows darkening and the night a great embrace, a connecting of all things.

The beast is what makes the man. We drink the blood of Christ so we can become animals again, tearing throats open and drinking blood, bathing in blood, devouring flesh, remembering who we are, reaching back and returning. We reassure ourselves. The Commandments impossible, and we can only fail, so we need this reassurance every Sunday that who we are has not been lost.

I swallowed that heart and was made whole. A generation completed, able to stand now before my father and grandfather. But there was more still to do. Dominion not yet complete. What made the buck a man needed to be removed also, and this the trickiest part, especially in failing light, darkness falling quickly.

I picked up my knife and knelt before his crotch, pulled at a leg to spread him wide. Continued the cut from his belly down farther now to his anus. Grabbed his balls and pulled, then sliced in close with the knife, flung the balls into brush, scattering him into oblivion. Flayed that hide away across his inner thighs and pulled the sheath off his penis, leaving only the inner stump of it, thin and rat-like, all hide gone.

The flies thick now, small satellites in the faint light, a madness always to their sound, creating an urgency in me. I carved down through muscle toward the pelvic bone, careful slicing. I needed to find the bladder and not rupture it. Urine would spoil the meat.

I didn't understand how the bladder had become hidden away like this. What was the plan or reason? I carved but was not able to reveal it. Reached in with my fingers carefully behind the meat and in among the bones, a place distorted by feel, and searched blind, hoping it would be small and could be pulled out through the hole for the penis, but it was large and full and still warm.

My face in close, the flies landing on my cheeks and neck and I couldn't see what I was doing, darkness thickening and my hands buried inside the buck, but finally I was able to free the membranes around the bladder and felt it relax into my hand.

I cut carefully around the anus, then pulled everything out through the hole: the colon, bladder, and penis, which I had to push down into its own smaller hole with one hand while I pulled with the other, thin rat's tail disappearing.

I carried the entire assembly in both hands carefully and dropped it into the brush, away from the meat. Then I returned for the lungs, scooped out the frothy mess and tossed it into the brush handful by handful, feeling along the ribs for any I might have missed.

Well, my father said.

Yeah, Tom said. We should get the truck.

So the men left me. They walked up that fire road, apparitions receding, darker blots against the general darkness, and I was left alone. Scooped my hands in along the walls, but all was smooth now and drying out. My hands constricting as the blood dried on them, a tighter second skin.

I stood beside the buck and looked up at the sky, a deep blue, the stars appearing, north star low and bright. I was a man now. This fire road and slope a holy place, the sacrifice made, rituals performed. But it was better than that. I wish I could return to that moment. A new beginning, a kind of innocence, the old life and self burned away. Isn't this what we all want? And how many times do we experience it in a life? The moment never lasts long enough.

All was whole. This place I stood the only place, and this buck on the ground beside me my buck, and I had done what was required, my work finished, and the only light from this deep blue and the stars, no sign of other humans except this road, a swath cut into the brush, but if I could forget that and erase it then I could have been standing in any time, and this hillside and even the sky above belonged to me. I remember I spread my arms wide that night and felt I could extend infinitely. If I closed my fists and pulled inward, I could warp mountains, collapse ridges. All of this world within my grasp.

That night was mine. The men would walk up the fire road, take the fork to the sugar pines and the truck. We'd drive to camp and hang my buck head down alongside the dead man and I'd flay the hide from around the hams and punch my fist between hide and meat. I'd do this in lantern light, and dinner would be late, and I'd fall asleep exhausted. I hadn't slept during the afternoon nap or the night before. I lay back against the earth and could feel myself drifting off already, sleep an enclosure, muting all, but then I heard the truck start up, muffled and far away.

I stood and felt dizzy. No food, no water, no sleep. And the struggle with the buck, having to wrestle and cut through his neck with my knife. Shoulder sore from being slammed against the ground. Poison oak spreading everywhere, a plague. I kept scratching, and that only made it worse.

I could see the tops of high trees far away illuminate for a moment in headlights. Trees farther up the mountainside, above the glades. The growl of the truck very faint. This ridge a kind of bow, blocking my view and burying sound, distorting sound to the point that the truck seemed only more and more faint. And then I saw white on treetops again farther up the mountain, and this was not right.

The cutover to this fire road was at the top of the glades, not higher. The headlights should not have been facing away. They should have been sweeping the air above me and backlighting the ridge and the sound coming closer.

What are you doing? I said aloud. The sound of the truck no longer constant but only momentary, interrupted, fading.

They were leaving me. My father and grandfather and Tom were driving back to camp without me and without my buck.

I searched for my rifle, found it still snagged, freed it and wiped the dirt and blood on my jeans. Then I ran up that fire road, no moon, very dark now, the road a slightly lighter black against darker black, an image against my eyelids when I blinked. No hope of catching them, but I ran anyway because there was nothing else I could do.

Heaving up that hill, legs burning, scraping against brush at the side then veering until I was at the top of the bow, where the mountain fell inward and the road leveled out, and I saw the white of the headlights far away on another slope, faint illumination of brush, and a wink of red.

I levered a shell into the .30–.30 and fired at where I had seen the taillights. I didn't think about it. I just fired. I was so angry. And the rifle kicked back hard against my shoulder. Not something I had felt firing at the buck, but now I knew the full jolt of it, unprotected by the thrill of killing, and my ears blanked out and I smelled sulfur and the truck kept moving, unaffected.

I stood there breathing hard. I couldn't hear a thing, only the static of my own head welling up.

Marooned on this hillside, abandoned by my kind. The dark bulk of the mountain rolling beneath me. The brush all around a malevolence, watching and waiting.

I was too angry to move. Just frozen with it, in disbelief.

But the truck wasn't coming back. It had vanished into another fold, and the temperature was falling fast, and I was wearing only a T-shirt and the buck was laid out on the road and it was miles back to camp.

I didn't know what to do, but I walked back down the road to the buck. There was no other option. I would need to try to carry the buck to camp.

I found him in the road, a shadow against other shadows, this night without a moon, and I knelt in front of the cavity, careful to avoid the pile of entrails. I felt around in the dirt for my knife, having to crawl like a blind man, my fingers sifting dust until I found the blade. I wiped it on my jeans and then I reached for his hind legs. The Achilles tendon and sack of musk, bitter and maddening, and I sliced the gap between bone and tendon, a natural hollow covered by nothing more than thin hide. I cleared both legs in this way then reached for the forelegs. These I snapped at the elbow, broke until the bone jutted out, and I slipped each foreleg through a hindleg, making a backpack. Those jutting bones slipped through and caught on the Achilles tendons.

My knife sheathed and rifle in hand, I lay down beside the buck, my back against his belly, and slipped his hooked legs over my shoulders, pulled his neck and head and antlers over my chest, cradled in close. Then I pushed up off the ground to a sitting position and struggled to stand.

The buck weighed more than I did. Maybe

a hundred and twenty pounds, even without the guts, and the weight was the same as stone. Hard and unyielding and real. I took a step forward up that hill, and another, and my legs were shaking, my back caving. There was no way I could do this for a couple miles.

I did try. I kept moving, hunched forward and pulling and placing one leg and then another. His head and antlers thumping against my chest, a new kind of beast fused with man, walking together and sharing the same breath and blood. Hollowed out, but hide and hooves and antlers shielding the bareness and weakness of man. And what would I become? If I made it all the miles to camp, would I gain hooves?

I believed this animal could become me. I felt that. I was a child still, and so none of the boundaries of this existence were set. All was possible. Metamorphosis. Desire and will and despair strong enough to change physical form and find a truer shape. My legs thinned at the calves and feet hardening, shrinking, and my thighs strengthening and rotating at the joint. A ridge across the top of my skull and bone growing, my neck thickening against the weight. Hair across my arms more coarse and dense and matting, skin toughening into hide. All sound magnified, coming closer, minute and exact, scent of every plant distinct, eyes finding light in shadow. All thought gone and replaced by the world. The immediacy and enormity of that world, and to become a part of it, finally, no longer removed. The curse of humanity is to lose the world, thought the loss of immersion.

No doubts, no indecision, only instinct. I was something entirely other than the buck. And the night was not immediate to me. I did not know every sound and movement, could not smell most of what was in the air. I had no hide to shield me.

If I could have transformed, I could have carried that weight. But I remained human and weak and faltered and fell sideways onto the ground, onto the buck, this backpack of flesh still warm.

I pushed his head and antlers away and slipped free of his legs and stood and didn't know what to do. The night black, truly black, the stars bright above but somehow casting no light on the ground. A separation of impossible distances, this lower world lost to the light.

I grabbed those horns and pulled the buck, dragged him across the ground, uphill. Walking backward, stooped over, pulling with everything I had, wandering over this dark earth dragging a dead body limp and heavy.

Hell not what we think of, populated and

busy, torments everywhere and flames, figures hopping this way and that to distract and entertain. Hell will be solitary. Each of us dragging across an endless dark expanse, featureless. Hell will be an endless task. Nearly impossible to drag this body even a few more feet, my back in agony, and yet this will go on for a night entire, and then a confusion of nights and time lost and years passing and lifetimes and finally geologic time, the surface shifting beneath my feet, mountains rising and forming and wearing away and still this dragging and each moment too much, each moment unbearable. Hell is time refusing to pass and the enormity of it waiting still to be passed.

The body we drag in hell is our own, all that we've been and the weight of that, pulling backward and not seeing where we're going, same as when we lived. Directionless, blind, pointless. Our suffering not building to anything, refusing meaning. Only dragging on.

The body catching on root and scrub and rock, snagging. Having to heave and yank but with no back left and thighs burning, and when the weight drags again it has gained resistance, the ground a gatekeeper, refusing passage.

Our sight will be the first sense to go in

hell, because it was most precious to us in life. We'll have it only long enough to see the stars above and learn their distance. We'll spend some endless number of nights believing they might come closer, believing we might reach them. We'll come to rely upon them as a consolation, and without meaning to we'll begin thinking of them as a goal. They'll offer escape, another place, and then they'll seem fainter, less distinct, and this will last long enough we won't be able to remember whether the stars were ever more distinct but our desire for them won't have lessened, and then they'll suddenly be gone entirely, just gone and no light anywhere and we won't know whether we're still able to see or not. We'll want to rub at our eyes, poke and prod and try to bring them to life, but our hands will not be free.

We'll focus then on sound, the dragging of this body over rough earth. And because we'll have nothing else, we'll make a world of that sound. A scuff of hide over dirt all I could hear on this hillside, a heft and weight general and entire, but then sound separates and small stones shift beneath and roll and grind against outcrops of stone, small ridges like spine protruding, ripping at the hide, sound of tearing, and we can't know what we're dragging, an animal with stiff hairs or our own bodies because the sound of tearing is a sound of fear and can't be known. Hooves over the ground, we should be able to hear those, some track they make, but the dirt in millions of grains and hundreds of small stones and momentary drag across tufts of grass and scrape against root and brush are so many sounds all at once we become lost. Sound itself a landscape of hell, no escape at all, and now we're dragging in two worlds that grow further apart, world of touch and world of sound, the body we drag no longer indicated and perhaps not our own.

Touch. Physical weight and strain, and this endless night colder and colder, all warmth fading and the sun never to rise again. Muffled world, blind and soundless, but not detached. Pain and nowhere else to focus but on that pain. The failure of the body, grinding of bone against bone, splitting of muscle, and nerves light up our dark sky. We have some sense of seeing again, but this time inside us, bright spots of grinding and tearing that race in slim lines, impulse and pattern, red network of pain, and seeing this removes us from it, limits what we feel, and we think we can manage, but then all goes dark again and now we know every pattern, every raceway, but only feel its surge, don't see a thing. Pain. The sensation of pain, always fresh. And there is no other sense. Taste and smell never mattered during our lives, and they don't matter in hell. We've forgotten them. And though we continue to walk backward, dragging this weight, we no longer know because we've become lost inside ourselves, each hell private and contained.

The night cold, the air sinking around me. I could feel it thin as it chilled, and I wanted some shield from it. Dragging that buck my only way of generating heat, but my strength was failing. Pulling in short yanks now, no longer able to keep the movement unbroken.

The buck was too large. I held those antlers and pulled but the rest of him was a weight formless and extending, the back half of him invisible to me now and fusing with the ground, sending shoots into the earth and anchoring. Flesh become root and curling around rock. No way to dislodge him. Grown in darkness, black sun.

This night a day that I could not see. His neck stretched as I pulled, his body elongating and springing back. My steps reaching nowhere and all reference gone. Eternity.

I was not going to make it. Shivering now in the cold, clammy from chilled sweat, my T-shirt thin. I dropped his antlers, a hollow sound that came from somewhere else, directionless, my body tilting, and set the rifle down carefully in that rack, where I would not lose it, and unsheathed my knife. I had to

198

sever the back half of him, the part rooted in the ground, and I had to work quickly.

I knelt before him and cut through hide and flesh at the lower edge of his rib cage, where he was thinnest. Pulling the flesh taut and yanking upward with the blade.

Thick muscles of his back, pushing until blade met bone. I stood and leaped over him, become nimble in the darkness, same as any imp or devil, and kicked his spine. His back rubbery and resistant as a root, impossible to crack. So I knelt and took the knife in both hands, blade up, stabbed low into thick muscle, tore upward.

He was shifting in the darkness, changing shape, not wanting to be severed. The slope rolling beneath us, becoming steeper, and I held on to that knife, digging a trough.

The night colder and colder, the sun never to rise, flesh severed and thickening and severed again, and I seemed to make no progress. His back an endless thing, and so I must have been tearing holes all along it. But finally I came to bone, and placed my hand over his spine and there was no meat on either side and I could feel the rough discs laid one on another.

I kept my hand in place, my one reference in that night, and fit the tip of the knife into a seam between discs. All that we can know housed in bone. Every image, memory, thought, and touch cabled in bone and easily pried apart. The mechanics of what we think is a soul. Hell a place where all is dismantled, all laid bare, all reduced to blood and bone and flesh gone dead, pieces of us lying in darkness never to form again. Working my knife side to side and feeling the discs separate, a gap forming, stabbing deeper into that cord that connects us to the world or perhaps creates it.

We don't know what makes life. Spine and brain hooked up to a pump and oxygen, but that's not enough. We can put all these parts back together forever and never make a thought, and perhaps this is our task in hell, to try to build what we had taken for granted. Feeling our way across the ground searching for some missing piece, some hunk of discarded flesh that will provide a spark.

I stabbed into that spine and wedged the blade until all was severed and lost and only a few ribbons of meat left to attach one half of him to the other. I sawed quickly at these, my knife digging into the ground, and finally was free.

I was quick to grab my rifle and pull at those horns, before he could grow together again or root his upper half. Lighter now, half his weight gone, dragging again over the earth. Still heavy enough I had to pull with both hands, stepping backward, my rifle wedged between his antlers.

Veering into brush, scraped along my side, angling back again, my heels digging, the sound of him like canvas, that hide thick. Dragging and dragging in darkness, and the sound of this dragging became everything. Never continuous but separate with each footstep, delayed and burdened, shortened and he grew heavier, managed to expand somehow or increase in density. Sixty pounds, maybe, dead weight, but it felt like more than that, and I hadn't known this road was so long. Not even at the fork yet, at the top of the glades. First cold breath of air coming up the road toward me, no longer still.

No heat left, and the air coming to take whatever might remain. My back bowed and gone rigid. Looking down I thought I could see his eyes, some greenish light at the back of them, some night vision luminescent still, faint enough I might only be imagining it, vanished in a blink, but then there it was again, faint galaxy of stars far away, green or perhaps blue, and there were two galaxies, both eyes because I held his antlers so that he was facing me, as if we would meet and I would always pull him closer as I retreated.

The two of us hung in space, satellites

around some center not yet discovered, the mountainside lurching beneath us. Rotating faster and I could not see anything except those two universes bright and faint as dreams, the charms of hell, meant to distract, promises from the deep. Attached to a great weight that was ending me.

He was growing again, sending down roots again, invisible in darkness, long thick shoots into the earth as we dragged more and more slowly across the ground, all hidden by this distraction, and then I caught the outward tracer, the quick orbit of a fly. The sound of it sudden and far too loud, and I wondered if it had been there all along. I didn't know. Visible now, and others also in their arcs like shooting stars, a green-blue that matched the light from deep inside the buck's eyes, an ethereal light, promise of heaven, an endless trick in hell.

No flies in darkness. Another trick. They were meant to sleep and wait for day. Eyes large and made of many small mirrors of light. The buck had become what fed upon him. These eyes of his not his at all.

I panicked now, dropped his antlers and my rifle and ran up that dark channel careening into brush: scrub oak, chamise, coyote brush, buckbrush, all the inventions of Hades. Fingers ridged and clumped and sharp and reaching toward me. I was eleven years old, only eleven, and the terrors I could imagine were not yet limited but were closer to their sources. That buck a demon that could conjure other demons and warp the world.

I pulled my knife, and I cut at the air, spun in that blackened road and ripped at all that came up from behind. Blade finding nothing, and that was more frightening still. Lunging at vacuums, shadows that breathed in close and vanished.

You could say this is what I've been doing ever since, in all these years, that nothing has changed, this moment suspended infinitely, repeating. But meanwhile the world has ratcheted on, each action following the next as if all would lead somewhere.

I walked back down to the buck, stepping slowly, not able to see the ground, feeling my way as if at the edge of some cliff, the ocean below, arms out and knife still ready. Steeper ground than I remembered, a fall with each foot and then scrape of dirt and rock and feel of my fingers against nothing.

The buck waiting. Clung to the earth and burrowing into rock, rib and spine and flesh grafting into plant form, rigid cell walls, plunging downward, digging, grafting into mineral, walls hardened and hardening still, fault lines and ruptures reaching below where I stood now. I had very little time.

I needed to sever that neck. That was the only way. Sever the neck, grab his antlers and my rifle and run.

Empty, ragged gap at his throat, cut through to bone. Thick muscle behind this. I knelt again at this altar, every altar in the afterlife a place of blood and butchery, just as in life, and I sliced through hide and into flesh, carving down through everything I could not see. Waiting for the knife to hit stone, the metamorphosis. Neck turned to stone that would enclose my knife and lodge it there forever, reach upward into my hand and bind. The feel of my own flesh crystallizing, blood gone rigid, caught in this act and held. What does it mean when we turn to stone?

I dug through that neck as quickly as I could until I heard metal on bone and wrapped the knife around, cutting everything that might still be hidden. I grabbed the antlers then and yanked backward hard. Cracking sound, and I yanked again and twisted and then I dug that blade between vertebrae and stabbed and finally severed.

A severed head. I couldn't help but look at the buck's eyes and see that they were still galaxies entire, made of some substance that wouldn't fade, a luminescence beyond blood. The buck not diminished.

I was careful not to let his open neck touch ground. As long as I kept him aloft, he would not root again. I held his antlers with one hand at my shoulder and let his eyes look up into the sky. I knew not to look longer at them.

Heavier than I ever would have dreamed, that head and neck and antlers, and I had to stoop over to pull up that road, and the weight was too much for one hand. Dead weight of flesh, our bodies so much heavier than we imagine.

I wasn't sure what to do, standing in place bent over and breathing hard, my shoulder burning, but I slipped the rifle barrel up until it lay across my shoulders and then I could grab the antlers with both hands.

If anyone could have seen me in that darkness, it would have looked as if I was trying to wear his head and horns, trying to pull them in place of my own, bent over and become any beast, hiding away from mankind.

Jesus in the desert, forty days in wilderness, going back, refusing civilization. His feet hardening into hooves, ears tufting, a ridge grown across his head and sockets for horns, bone growing, and he leans over onto his forelegs and finds an easier stride. Able to pick his way among the rocks, dainty of foot, ready to leap and run at any threat. The hide thickening across his back and shielding him from the relentless sun. Galaxies forming at the backs of his widened eyes, luminescence, night vision, a second day.

Our stories of transformation have been taken, erased from the Bible we have now. Where is Pan, half goat, with a man's torso and goat's horns? Where are the mermaids, half fish? Where is Medusa with her head of snakes? These stories are a part of us and can't be erased. The Bible isn't finished until what was erased has been returned.

Jesus was hiding. And what do any of us have to hide except the beast? Hooves and antlers and the world returned, a landscape animate. Jesus as aurochs, the bull, thick dark horns, shaggy hanging head thundering across desert stone. Or gone down lower onto his belly, thick toes ending in points, tongue flicked outward to smell, platelets all along his back, eyes like beads.

Scent of the buck on me. Smell also of blood. Bent over to face the earth invisible below, stepping into that darkness.

The spine in us comes from fish, the first vertebrate fish. And our legs and arms are fins. This is truth. The lungfish is more closely related to us than he is to most fish. He breathes air, walks across dry land, burrows in to wait for rain, lives as long as we do. Jesus in the desert, going back to his origins, would have seen his arms and legs shrink back into lobed fins, felt his tail regrow and complete the ridge of his back. He would have burrowed down into the earth and dreamed of water.

Waiting and wandering and migration, all forgotten. I climbed that hill spine curled and strained and carrying my trophy, and I did not stop. We can return to that. One foot in front of the other even when we have no strength, even when we need to sleep and need food and need water. We can continue on anyway.

The earth could have been flat. If it was created, then why not any shape? So gravity and steep hillsides must be meant as torments, a test of us. That hill rose before me, and my steps were not entirely solid but slipped back a bit, and brush tore at my face until I veered away, and then scraped from the other side and I veered again. I couldn't see. The buck staring into the heavens and all illumined for him. If the world evolved, then it is what it is. If it was created, then its shape is the inferno.

The sound of my footsteps and nothing more. Slow plodding, and after a while it seemed they could have been someone else's footsteps, sound dislocated. I listened to this other figure hike along that road. Always near and out of reach. A phantom you could forget and then remember again. Each step isolated, pushing, carrying something. No momentum. A sound made of will alone.

Hell an echo chamber, all without source. Our preview in this life is our sense of self, never constant, no solidity, nowhere to be found. A kind of shadow projected out over this brush and changing constantly in size, and the light that makes that shadow something beyond the range of what we can see. We know the shadow is there but can never find it.

A scraping sound, this was all I heard at first. But then a low thud beneath it, my weight against the earth, proof. Cast just to my side, walking in tandem. And then slipping farther away and behind. My skin, also, a separate thing, overgrown by the oak and hung beyond the outlines of me.

The gun a rack across my neck, cold steel, and the buck's antlers bloodless. His upper vertebrae against mine, two-headed creature looking opposite directions, earth and sky, our eyes mounted to the sides. A guardian impossible to approach. A single set of lungs, single breath.

At times my heartbeat felt doubled, a reverberation as it hung and shook in my chest. Wave pattern rippling outward, some relation to the thud of each footstep, no low sound ever contained, always reaching beyond.

The road rising more steeply at the top of the glades. My toes digging in like hooves. Strange calves, too thick. No calves on a buck, only slim bone and tendon, all muscle up high. Our proportions are wrong, feet too large and swiveling.

I hit brush in front of me, a wall of it, closed and blind, fully grown, and so I knew I was at the fork. I could see nothing at all, not even when I blinked and looked for outlines, but I turned to the right and felt the hump in the center of the road beneath me, covered in short brush, and stepped to the side into a wheel rut.

I followed this trough, lugging that head. My elbows up, shoulders burning, tiny compared with the shoulders of a buck. Huge sweeps of muscle, able to leap, but they lay now in the road behind, disconnected. A pair of forelegs and shoulders and rib cage and section of spine wandering on their own, resting for a moment, lying down in the road. And farther down that road, another pair of legs unable to pull or drag, only pushing flesh into ground, going nowhere.

I couldn't risk being overtaken, had to keep moving. My footing uncertain beneath me, deep channeled rut carved by water. Large stones uncovered and gathered at the seam, and my feet slipping along the walls. In darkness, I wouldn't know how deep. I could be following a channel that cut until the hill on either side was over my head or even higher and I wouldn't know. Submerged and believing I was still on the surface.

But the slope became less steep, walls lay down and rut filled. Shallow curve of ground, smell of sugar pines and sound of air moving through their tops, the road no longer a channel, and the toe of my boot kicked an enormous cone and I stepped on another, crunching down through it, and I was where my grandfather had gathered his cones.

I had to rest a moment. Went down on my knees in soft needles and grass and tilted to the side to let the rifle butt hit ground and head fall. I pushed cones out of the way and curled into a fetal position, first and final form. Breathing hard. The ground already cold, all warmth of the day gone.

Here is where they had decided to leave me, knowing I might not make it back, knowing the buck would be wasted on the road. I wondered what had been said. They might have said nothing. They might have just climbed into the truck and left.

I didn't know them, and they didn't know me. All familiar shapes can become unfamiliar. One of the tricks of this world is the feeling that we belong.

All we have is necessity. I got up from that ground because I was cold, and I would walk again because camp was the only refuge. I heaved that head and rifle again onto my back and tried to find my way in darkness.

The road no longer well defined. My feet sifting through grass and the ground become uneven and almost immediately I was lost. This was no road. I stood in place, listening, as if the road might speak, and tried to find some internal compass, some sense of whether I had strayed to the right or left. The air curling around me, always a confusion, always misleading. The air is where the devil does his tricks.

But of course there is no devil. We only

want there to be. We want someone in charge. Hell is anarchy, each of us in charge of everything and nothing and hearing no other voices ever. Isolation more terrifying than punishment.

If I chose the wrong direction, I would be twice lost and turned around and never find my way back. I cut to the left but stayed low to the ground, dragging the buck's head and the rifle, sweeping my free hand over grasses, feeling their tops, searching for a hollow, a place where the grass had been flattened.

My palm a diviner, searching for disruption, for a track in the void. My eyes closed, as if that might help. Closed against the darkness. Reaching back to some earlier knowledge of air and ground.

And the air did cave, and my hand swept down, and the flattened grasses formed a faint track, and I rose again, too tired to lift the head, holding antlers in one hand, heavy and slumped, my rifle in the other. A figure shuffling alone in darkness in a dry place of thorn and scrub, carrying a severed head and a gun. How could that not be a landscape of hell? And it had duration, also, an infinite time on that road, climbing the slope and traversing and falling repeatedly off the track into spines.

I don't know what the devil would look like

if he did exist. I think he would have my face, but I know the rest of him would take a different form, and that form could not be of only one beast but would be all the beasts we fear, foreign and corollary. You'd never be able to see the devil entirely, always some part of him shifting and hidden. He can never be outlined.

My grandfather was the closest form I knew, his face my own but deformed and soulless, his body shifting constantly and never seen in full, terrifying and capable of anything. He was close enough.

I shivered on that road and drew closer and closer to him, bearing my burdens like gifts. A severed head to placate the fiend and avoid annihilation for one more day.

And as I walked, a strange thing happened. I began to believe that I could see. The world illuminating just faintly, some internal light I could cast into the void, and then brightening into dark blue, and I realized it was the moon, hidden still behind mountains but turning one part of the horizon white, outlining ridges and peaks far away across the valley.

The road visible now, all forms of the air receding, all become thin, no longer frightening. I hiked faster, trying to warm, desperately cold, my teeth clacking and shoulders bent down and stretched. I knew where I was now, and not far left to go.

Falling forward, stumbling, the road clear, the land flattening and space opening up among the trees waiting on this hillside, a stillness to them, a great calm, a reassurance. Grown in parallel, all knowing the same warp of the earth. The world returned. Vacant mountain, no demons here.

The moon a stationary thing as it moved. Solid and near. Light soft, indirect, and all revealed, the ferns of the reservoir and wild grape climbing all along that bank, shape-shifting, large leaves in mounds and trellises, filling every gap and hollow, a kind of blanket to cover deadfall and rut.

I was the only demon here, my cargo a form of blasphemy in that peaceful night, scuttling along, hunched and burdened. Rushing now, almost running, and I looked over my shoulder, felt that I was followed, some other part of my own self, feeling too exposed now in the light, needing cover.

Running, those horns bumping at my thigh, nose swinging into my knee, the rifle solid in my other hand. Passing beneath ponderosa pines, the small dark shapes of their cones above me against the whitened sky. Up rises and around curves and down across flats, more contour than I had ever realized in the truck, the land growing, but I was gaining.

Scrape of my boots loud but I felt I could outrun anything now, and I pounded up the final draw toward camp, steeper than I had remembered, and hit the open space just before our grove.

I slowed here and went down on my knees, dropped the head and lay in the dust of the road with my rifle as I had the previous night, waiting and listening for any sign of my grandfather. Breathing hard, winded, and my blood pounding, but I waited until I could calm and hear. He had no relation to the ground. That was the problem. Those pencil legs without sound, and the orb of him above that, able to shift anywhere. You wouldn't know what you were seeing or hearing until too late.

The heat falling away from me again, and I could find nothing, and my skin slick now with sweat and chilling. The trees before me, thick grove in which the men slept and the dead man waited. I rose with the antlers and left the road, followed the stream. The meadow just beyond was another moon, luminous and white.

The dead man hanging without his sack, banded by shadows. Hanging from his bare and bloodless ankles. I could see him and then not see him and then see him again as he shifted through those trees.

The sound of the water a camouflage he was using. I could not hear his movement, only the stream, endless. A sound growing as I neared, taking over until I could no longer hear even my own blood and breath. Trees rotating on their bases across the ground, as if all were held on a great dial. Some low sound to that, deep tumblers of stone, but it could have been only the water, a heavier fall into a deeper pool.

His chin ducked close against his chest, the tops of the trees his references, and he slid among them at will. This was the temptation, this is how the demon has always moved, never looking directly. Shadows everywhere around Jesus, and what he had to learn was that there was only his own.

I held the buck's severed head high as I entered those trees, held it before me as a shield, no beast here more terrifying than I could be. Those luminescent eyes, dead galaxies holding an afterlight, and the dead man could no longer slip away, veered and shifted and went nowhere, was held in place at the hooks and contained until I stood before him and the dial no longer moved beneath me and the trees rooted again.

My trophies, both of them, equivalent, no difference, and neither would be taken from me. I dumped the head on the ground and my rifle beside it. Loosened a rope and let another hook fall.

The men might hear this, and my grandfather could move as fast as any demon. But I felt some odd strength, invincibility almost, after all I had been through on that road. I didn't even glance behind. I only grabbed this hook and the head of the buck and looked for where to impale. No hind legs, no Achilles tendons, all abandoned. And not possible to violate one of those eyes. So I faced him away from me, caught between my knees, and reached around to hook him in the mouth, yanked back hard to drive that hook into his throat. Then I let him fall again and went to the trunk to raise the rope until his head dangled near the dead man's ankles, leaning in close to the dead man, nodding and looking down. Here they could ponder each other and wonder how each had come to be. Man staring into the heavens, buck gazing down from above.

Kicked awake by my father, still dark. He'd found my hiding place behind the fallen trunk. Get up, he said. Familiar shadow, made foreign now by my time on the road.

Exhausted and curled in my sleeping bag, I did not want to wake. Breath heavy. But he jabbed his boot in my side again and I sat up. Okay, I said.

Get over here, he said.

He walked away, backlit by a small fire, yellow outlines of him and a cavern forming above in the trees. Domed ceiling of any cathedral. The moon low on the other side of the sky now, setting, fading in firelight. No stained glass. No windows, even. Open arches.

My back in knots, but I rose and pulled on my jacket and hat and boots and followed him across shadows and deadfall, hollows and pools of black, carrying my rifle. The trees dry above, all color leached. My skin coming alive.

Tom at the griddle, a kind of Hephaestus I see now, working in darkness, without a lantern, working always with hot iron and

218

sizzling flesh, no longer forging in metal alone. My grandfather still on his slab of marble, but I thought I saw an eye open as I passed. My father gone beyond the fire to stand before the hooks, our altar.

Dead man and buck the same color, pale yellow, horns and ankles made of the same bloodless material. Almost as lifeless as the painted plastic hanging in any church.

You can't hang a man next to a buck, my father said.

That's all I have left of the buck. I had to leave the rest of him in the road.

They're not the same.

They are the same, my grandfather said from behind us. I turned and he was already up in his long johns, a mound of flesh wrapped loosely in cloth stained and yellowish in this light, his robes. As if we all had come here to be judged by him.

Don't start, my father said.

Well what is the difference? Your son has killed a man and a buck, and you and he have hung them here. You hung the man yourself. You skewered his ankles as if he was an animal.

They're not the same.

How are they not the same?

I'm not listening to this, Tom said. He walked over and was holding a spatula, the small fire close behind him, associated with him. Bright spots of grease along his bare forearm. We eat a buck. We bury a man. There's the difference, you fucking monster. He was pointing at my grandfather with the spatula, as if it were some kind of knife.

There's nothing left to eat, I said. You made me leave everything in the road.

My grandfather smiled. The best part of youth, he said. The utter lack of humor.

What does that mean? I asked.

Take that head down, my father said. I won't have them hanging together. My father's face creased in this light, long thin shadows down his cheeks. He was a weak figure. He could make no demands. He determined nothing, and this had always been true.

It's my first buck. I get to hang him here.

My father's arm a sequence too fast to follow, a kind of shadow that struck the side of my face and knocked me into the dirt. My skin burned and bones of my face throbbing. On my knees and still holding my rifle.

He's right, my grandfather said. He gets to hang his first buck here. That's the rule we follow. If we don't follow that, then why not eat the man and bury the buck?

And suddenly that's what I could see. On my knees on that ground, the blood still pumping in my face, I could see Tom carving pieces off the dead man and frying them on his grill. A different kind of church, the body of Christ more literal, no icon in wood or plastic but actual flesh and each of us feeding from it every day. Feeding from the flesh of bucks, too, and finding no difference.

You really are a monster, Tom said.

What rule says you eat the buck and not the man? my grandfather asked.

Every fucking rule in the world.

Did the rules say this boy could kill that man?

No.

Well what happens to the rules then?

Sometimes I think I invented my grandfather, that he never existed on his own. His voice is my own voice now, and I can't find any separation. I can't find what was him then and what is me now. His views have infected me.

You are all fucked in the head, Tom said. All three of you, and when we get back, everyone's going to know. Enjoy your last bit of craziness. We're leaving here today.

We're not leaving today, my grandfather said. We're going for a hunt today, and then taking a nap, and then going for another hunt, same as every other day. And we're leaving tomorrow, as we planned. And that buck's head is going to hang there until we leave.

We're not going for a hunt, my father said. I'm burying this man. I'm going to bury him right now. This has gone on too long. You can have your fucking head hanging there all you want, but the man is not hanging beside him.

My father went to the ropes then, worked in darkness, his back against the light, and I could hear the men breathing above me, could hear the snap of the fire.

Rope tearing against bark, and the dead man fell before me, all one piece in motion, a slab, no collapse or fold but only a hard dull fall onto his shoulders and then ankles swinging down slowly until they rested a few inches above the ground. Some part of him refusing to return to earth, something always otherworldly about him. Sly grin still and head ducked, capable of anything.

So you're ready to say this man's death meant something? my grandfather asked.

I'm not saying anything, my father said. And I'm not talking to you.

Well what does it mean to bury him?

You don't ask questions like that.

These are the only questions. What if we chop his head off and bury him with the buck's head? Does that make any difference?

Tom walked over to the fire and took out a long thick stick burning at its end. Red grid of coals inside the flames. He held this up and gazed at it. Would it matter if I burned your eyes out with this stick? he asked. Would that make any difference?

I'm not the one whose eyes should be burned out, my grandfather said, and he pointed down at me. If the man's death means something, then there has to be consequence.

Both of you, my father said. Please just kill each other now. I can't listen to either of you ever again.

What does it mean to bury him? my grandfather asked. What will that do?

The dead man was looking all around while we were distracted. Shifty-eyed. Planning his escape. A quick leap over the stream, through trees and ferns and into that meadow. Head of a buck, body of a man, feet swiveling and flapping at the earth, arms yanking at his sides useless, but that great head with its rack and large eyes looking back, seeing all shapes. Body jerking below, but that head smooth, gliding over the earth.

My father crawled to the ankles and pulled them to ground, yanked out the hooks. The dead man free now, and I waited for him to run, but my father rose and picked up the ankles with their bloodless holes and dragged him toward the truck. The man's arms outstretched and knuckles curled, risen off the ground, locked into that shape, reaching for everything, no neck, orangutan Jesus pale and rotting and waiting. He would not go into any grave easily. I knew that.

Well I guess it's back to bed, my grandfather said, yawning and scratching his sides. We come close, and then we just go on. Dig your hole and try not to think about anything.

Fuck off, my father said.

Yeah, my grandfather said. He turned and picked his way carefully over the needles and cones, barefooted, unsteady, and sat down at the table. Breakfast first, then I'll fuck off and catch a bit of shut-eye.

Tom tossed his firebrand back into the pit and returned to the griddle. Fine, he said. Aren't you going to ask any important questions, though? Why eat an egg? What is an egg? What does the egg have to do with the bacon? Is there any rule that says we have to eat the bacon before the egg? What if the bacon is the egg? Is there any consequence to an egg?

Help me lift him, my father said. He was talking to me, waiting at the back of the pickup.

I stood, but I didn't want to touch the dead man. I couldn't just reach down and hold those hands.

Right now, my father said. Hurry the fuck up.

My father in shadow, the truck blocking the fire. I held my rifle in both hands as I came closer and was hidden also. Cold and not yet morning.

Now, he said.

The dead man a pale bluish shadow against the darker ground. Those hands suspended and curled midair, warning us, trying to describe the enormity of something but frozen midwarning, without blood or sound or time.

Put down your rifle and grab his hands.

I was frozen, locked as solidly as the dead man.

Fuck me, my father said. He dropped the ankles and circled the dead man in only three quick strides, grabbed my arm and hauled me around to the feet. Grab his ankles then, he said.

The dead man reaching for me. Unclear where the ground was or which way we hung in gravity. It looked like he was standing above with those arms reaching high, which meant I was lying on the ground, the world rocked ninety degrees, but there was only air behind my back. I was held against nothing, and the dead man bearing down. His head ducked low because he was about to spring.

Grab his ankles. My father's voice loud.

The removal of Jesus from the cross. His

burial. The problem is that he's going to rise, and there's some premonition of that, and the premonition binds you in place. You can't move or breathe.

Goddammit, my father said. Are you completely fucking retarded?

Your son knows, my grandfather said from the table. He knows the man's death means something. He knows there's going to be consequence. He knows more than you do.

How about you dig a hole, my father shouted back. How about you dig a big hole and get down in it and when we get back we'll throw the dirt over. I'd be happy to do that. No hesitation at all.

You can't bury everything, my grandfather said. Some things won't be buried.

Spare me.

What will this burial do? Will it mean your son didn't kill the man? Will it mean the man's not dead?

Did the bacon come from the egg? Tom asked. Did the bacon ever have wings? Is the bacon a pterodactyl?

My father knelt down in darkness at the man's side and cradled him, lifted him in a drooping slab, arms and legs not quite rigid, and turned to swing the feet in first over the tailgate, but they weren't high enough, even with the tailgate down. They were caught.

Aaah! my father yelled, and he dipped and swung the body to get those feet to clear, then pushed the dead man into the bed with all my grandfather's pinecones, sliding him along metal ruts. The body pale and rubbery and flexing, a different luminescence. Hands hanging midair still, over the edge, but my father swung the tailgate up and slammed them.

Get in the truck, he said.

Bravo, my grandfather said. You're halfway to nothing.

My father grim. I climbed in the cab and he was hunched forward over the wheel. You have done this, he said. This is all because of you. So you're going to drag that body all the way to the upper glade and give him a proper burial.

The upper glade?

That's right. My father turned the ignition then and the engine was surprisingly loud, rough and pulsing, racing against the cold.

Grab the shovel, he said. Unless you want to dig a grave with your bare hands.

I walked to the fire pit, my grandfather and Tom both watching, and grabbed our camp shovel, hinged and small, army surplus. It would take forever to dig a grave with that.

But I climbed into the cab, and my father turned the truck around and swung onto the road, except there was no road to see and he

227

did not turn on the lights. He drove in darkness. We left the fire and its light almost instantly, and there was no other light to steer by, the moon down now and only a dim scatter in one end of the sky.

The sound of the truck isolated us from the rest of the world. Held together in this cab waiting for what would happen. And yet sound is all my father could possibly have used to navigate. The scree along one side to know he was at an edge, the snapping of small branches under the tires and then drifting back into smoother sound of dirt and small rocks and pinecones crushing, soft small grenades going off. Or perhaps he drove from memory, the shape of this road become a part of him.

A dark form beside me, a form I didn't know. I couldn't see him, and it seemed it had always been this way. My grandfather had erased him.

Falling through darkness, compression in the engine winding up high and my hand braced on the dash, and I couldn't see what was below. The dead man behind falling toward us, his arms outstretched.

What I know of my father is that he was moral. He wanted all to be made right. He would have remade us all, melted us down and recast us in a different mold. And this was why he had no chance. This was why he

228

was erased and I can never remember him now as anything more than a shadow beside me, some reminder of who I perhaps should have been but could never possibly have been. You can't undo your own nature, and the moral are always left helpless in the face of who we are.

Jesus had a pagan burial. A chamber with room for the afterlife, closed off by a great stone. A desert burial, used for thousands of years before him. Not the beginning of any story. All the others rose from the dead also, to drink from their golden cups and drive chariots and parade around with jewelry and servants. Death a busy place. The only difference was that Jesus moved the stone.

Jesus broke the law, broke the separation between living and dead. A collision of our two worlds, and it could only be catastrophic. Jesus released the dead into our lives, set all the dead wandering the earth, freed the wraiths and demons we fear now, invaded the world of the living with all the figures of the afterlife, all the figures of hell, freed from the pagan demonland of Hades. No river and boatman to separate us, and now when night falls we can feel them everywhere, their lungless breath.

God wanted this. He sent his only son as an invasion of the otherworld into ours. This is the story of Jesus. After thousands of years of separate worlds, we finally had to admit that the demonland was inside us, and so we told this story of Jesus moving that stone, opening the gate, flooding our lives with all that we are, sent by god, who is only our own will. Jesus is our recognition of the demon inside us, a recognition of the animal inside us, the beast. A recognition we wanted and needed.

My father believed still in our goodness. He believed we could make things right and keep the demonworld at bay, and so he was destined to struggle and suffer without end. He drove us on in darkness, falling into caverns and compacting into ruts and rises, scraped along both sides, high eerie screes along the body of the truck.

I held on and didn't know what would be. We could easily have gone off any edge and tumbled to our end. Some of the land around us nearly flat, but before the upper glades we'd be driving along drop-offs, long falls of hundreds of feet into rock and air, and I had no way of measuring where we were. I had lost all reference, same as that ancient boat trip into the lower world.

You'll bury him, my father yelled over the engine and scraping. You'll bury him and we'll never mention him again.

I think I knew even at the time, even at eleven years old, that nothing buried ever is gone.

The land remained dark, even as the sky became the blue of a gun barrel, hard and nearly black, even as the stars began to fade and I could see the trees against the heavens, rough shadows in the sky forming and falling away and forming again, sudden apparitions, still without reference.

You're going to dig down until your hands bleed, my father yelled. You're going to pay.

I just held on as we lurched through the end of that night. It's unclear what payment has ever done. Nothing has been undone. Every act has remained. What is it in us that makes us believe we can pay? This is a belief in some order, some accounting.

My father stayed perfectly on that road he couldn't see, followed its every twist and turn as every shape leered from above and fell behind, outran all that would cling or follow except, of course, the dead man, who followed just behind us.

The sky bluer, less black, and in addition to the dark branches of trees passing above I could see the woolly shapes of brush to the sides, could see contour of the land, of the mountain rising to our left. The high ridge that led all the way to the top of Goat Mountain, tapering here, reachable, and somewhere just below it the upper glade, a bare patch of grass that fell steeply into pines.

The highest open space, with a view out over everything. The dead man would have the million-dollar view, as the dead always have. We don't believe in death.

The road visible now as two pale tracks with a dark hump between, and the brush and trees vanished from my side. I looked down a long fall into nothing, an edge of the world. The twilight arrived just in time. Boulders and rock faces blue apparitions faint and shifting, pulling from below. A feeling I can remember now, one that has never vanished or diminished, that deep chasm and its tug at us.

My father did not ease off the gas, and he did not hug the uphill side but simply drove on, the tires inches away from the edge, and I must have been holding my breath and willing the truck to remain on its path until we curved to the left and away from this void into trees again, darkened and again nearly blind as we arrived.

I remained in the cab, holding my rifle. I did not want to touch the dead man.

My father came around and opened my door. You're going to do this, he said. You're going to do this right now. And I'll hold your rifle. You'll need both hands.

I did not want to give up my rifle.

Get out here now.

I couldn't move. This mountain the wrong place to be. But my father grabbed the front of my jacket and yanked me out. Held me upright in the dust and took the rifle. Tall, much taller than I was, looming over me, a giant without understanding. He did not seem weak. Made stronger without my grandfather near, each generation sapping the next.

I'll carry the shovel, too, he said, and he pushed me and I walked to the tailgate and let it down and the dead man's hands reached out. Enough light now in that blue dawn to see the hollow shape of him, thin and pale. With his head ducked and arms up where he could not see, he looked like a child asking for help, asking to be lifted.

Touching the dead. We're not supposed to touch the dead. This is why we make a comfortable afterlife for them, so they will not reach out. We hope to distract them, keep them busy. Burial is a hope.

Grab his wrists and pull him out.

I can't do that.

You killed him. So now you bury him.

I can't touch him.

My father levered a shell into the .30–.30, a sound so loud I suddenly realized how quiet it was. A few small birds, light wings and leaves, an occasional chirp and nothing more.

The sky changing from dark blue to a lighter blue did not make any sound.

My father pressed the end of the barrel into my neck. You're my son, he said. I'm here to help you. I'm trying to figure out what the hell you are and trying to keep you from becoming that. But if you don't grab those wrists now, I'm going to pull the trigger.

Cold metal against my neck, pressing in, and a hollow I could not feel but the bullet would travel down that hollow and rip through my neck in an instant so fast it could not be known, and I did believe my father would pull the trigger. He had been pushed too far.

So I grabbed those wrists, cold and mostly bone, and felt the dead man's curled fingers on my forearms, his fingernails the same as any beak or claw or horn, the part of us made of something other than flesh, the part we want to deny, the reminder. I pulled and was afraid he'd separate, just rip in half, but all of him slid, and he did not complain or say anything at all, and I yanked again and he slid out until I was stepping backward quickly and he was falling, the weight of him off the end of that gate, and I could not let him fall on me, jumped back and let go as he landed hard.

The sound magnified in this bend of road,

under these trees. The dead man sly still, waiting for the right moment to make his move. Different from the buck, not rooting into the earth but trickier.

Not far from here was where he had begun, a living man sitting on that rock. Dragged downhill by my father. Dragged again by my grandfather across the meadow at the edge of our camp, and dragged back by my father to be hung a second time. Our lives repetition, not only us but all who came before, and Jesus, too, dragging his cross, form of suffering, form of a human life. In all our stories, we drag and scrape a weight across this earth. Called the Passion. Jesus a story of our pity for ourselves.

Get moving, my father said, as all fathers have said, enforcers generation after generation, slaves on every road.

So I grabbed those hands, fingerclaws scraping the underside of my wrists, and pulled him, and he slid more easily than the buck but was heavier, even hollowed out. He could not return to the earth. His connection had been severed. No root to burrow down, no transformation into plant or rock. The buck elemental still, made of the same material as the stars and trees. But the dead man heavier and heavier, accumulation of weight, gravity hole.

My heels digging into that loose slope of pine needles and leaves and fallen twigs over dirt, catching on rock beneath and the next step slipping again. Dragging in heaves backward, all movement shortened, my pull at one end become only inches of progress, all of him expanding and contracting and slipping back down and I didn't see how I would ever make it to the upper glade.

The dead man with his heels together, maintaining perfect form, swaying back and forth, a diver coming up from the depths or descending still.

Damn it, my father said, and he yanked one of the dead man's hands from me and pulled hard up that slope.

I scrambled to keep up, pulling with my right hand and clawing at the hill with my left, bent over low and toes digging in.

The dead man pooling all his weight now, hanging back and not wanting this burial, resisting a second death. Removed from the surface of the earth and sent into darkness, mouth filled with dirt and all light extinguished. Grains compacting above, layer upon layer, and no way to swim back through this, held down and drowned for eternity and lost. After Jesus invaded the world with the dead, we've been trying to keep the new dead from rising, the Christian burial no longer a

237

chamber but only a thick layer of dirt, a barrier.

The light flooding the sky now a cruelty, a reminder, false promise. The beginning always shown to us at the end. The sunrise behind this ridge. We would remain in shadow. But the stars were gone and the sky a milky blue, without distance or depth. Even this blue a lie and no longer a promise, and the blue removed from every other thing.

Brown of the pine needles, each bundle of three thin spears curving and held together by a wrapping of darker brown. My face in close. Orange tint to the underside of each spear. My mind needing to focus on something other than the weight and labor.

Scab leaves dry and loose, every light shade of brown. Bracken fern and bedstraw. Wild raspberry low and creeping along the ground, rare green. Male pinecones scattered everywhere, thin and brown and dried out, fallen from the lower parts of the trees, their yellow-green pollen shed, like used sparklers on Fourth of July.

That other world, of other people, lost and far away. Only the two of us here, and the two in camp, and no other humans. The life I inherited was this, and I had no power to change it. There was only the land, and human life no more than rumor. Two plants can graft and grow together, sharing water and nutrients, but not two people.

We hauled that body up the slope, tearing into the ground with our boots, and what I had was endless. Acorns fat and shiny, the crowns covered with yellow dusty hairs. Gold cup oak, or canyon live oak. This was all my father taught me. Not how to live with others or who to be but only how to see, and only this particular place of chaparral and oak and pine, a place lost to me now, and some days I want to shake my small apartment like a cage and break free and run back to where I belong, but I can't do that, of course. The dead man took everything away.

We moved too quickly up that slope. We charged at everything, and never slowed down, all that would happen determined by momentum alone. We were crazy with outrunning something that could not be outrun. Wherever we ended up, we were still there. We never seemed to understand that what we had to fear was carried inside us. The Greeks understood this, twenty-five hundred years ago, but we've forgotten.

That mountain a living thing, and we rose over its flank into the stand of gray pines at the base of the upper glade. My throat burning and skin slick. Blood pulsing even at the backs of my eyes, legs shot. But we didn't stop. Normally we'd stay low to the ground here, sneak quietly through trees looking for bucks on open slopes above, but this time we huffed and heaved and broke into the open pulling this weight.

The slope steep, seeming almost to overhang, outcrops of dark rock, shelves of grass and the world tilted, curled back over us. My father dragged me and the dead man up a central draw, dragged us through medusahead that looked almost like wheat but could snag in animals' noses and ears and clung to the laces of our boots, pale barbs.

We traversed then, slipping across that open fall onto a shelf that jutted out and rose high enough to see all the way to the top of Goat Mountain. Everything else lay below, a clear view of everywhere we had been and on across the far valley to the mountains on the other side, mountains everywhere and no human habitation, only a few thin scars of roads.

My legs were trembling as I stood in place, no power left in them.

Well, my father said. This is as good a place as any. In view of where you shot him, but fuck it. I don't care anymore whether we get caught.

I could see the stone where the poacher had sat, lower along the ridge. In shadow, and

I couldn't see blood from here, but I knew that was the stone, no more than two hundred yards away.

The flat where we stood not much bigger than what you'd need for a tent. The dead man lying on his back still, arms up, not caring where we stopped. Here was fine. He was an easy dead man most of the time, heavy as a sack of bricks but short on demands. He was in the way at the moment, though, lying right where I'd need to dig. There were a few maggots on the white-gray curve of his belly, come up through the bullet hole. Moving along but rolling to the side, a maggot always directionless, roving blind, dreaming of those eyes with their thousand mirrors, inheritance.

My legs were buckling, so I sat, but my father yanked me to my feet.

You don't get to rest. Grab those hands and we'll pull him upslope a bit. Then you dig.

Maggots, I said.

I know there are maggots. And maybe you should have to look at them.

My father put his boot under the man's back and heaved him over, face gone and I realized I hadn't taken a last look. I needed to see his face again. But all we had now was that cavern of hundreds of small white maggots crawling over each other hunting for flesh. No longer iridescent with flies, no longer beautiful, gone soundless and flat. The future we have to look forward to, learning to hear the chewing of a maggot, devoured slowly by everything that writhes, waiting for an afterlife that happened only once, when Jesus moved that stone, and isn't coming again.

My father left me there with the body and shovel, but he took the gun. He hiked uphill into short brush and then exposed rock and climbed along the spine of Goat Mountain, great chunks of broken rock like vertebrae leading up to that wide bald summit, the head, a thick plate meant for ramming, studded with outcrops that might as well have been horns. My father smaller and smaller, receding into the distance until he was no more than an ant on the larger vertebrae, disappearing in crevices and emerging again, the beast become larger toward the head.

The wide open slope where I stood would be the pelvic bone, and this seemed right for the place to bury the dead man, to bury him where he had been born. The goat a favorite form of the devil, the devil half man, half goat, and able to give birth endlessly, unceasingly, to every hybrid form, and when he's filled the world with enough of his own shadows, he'll rise up. This spine will unlock and rip itself free from the lower slopes and all smaller stones will fall away. He'll shake that great head and free it too and then his pelvic bone will tilt upward and there will be legs below and this slope will find itself hundreds of feet in the air and the dead man buried and clinging here.

But no one knows when the devil will rise or why. Doesn't he already have everything he wants? It's hard to know what he would gain.

This ground made of rock. The shovel loose and small and stabbing in no more than an inch or two, my bones jolting, impossible task. I removed the dry grass and hint of soil and the small loose stones, creating a scab on this hill and nothing more, no depth. I knelt in the center of the scab and was only confused. The day brightening and my father gone along that spine, and the air warming.

The dead man was not helping. Facedown for a nap, tucked into that hill, not concerned by the colony in his back. Dreaming of his chariot and four horses, golden bridles and reins and gold curved all along his arms. Driving fast across the earth, but this is desert and there must be sand in great dunes, and as he tries to gallop up a dune, the wheels dig in, the hooves mire, and he's sinking and sinking in sand, whipping his horses and going nowhere. Or maybe this kind of dream stops when you're dead. Maybe the pressure and panic are gone.

The dead man was looking straight down

into the earth. His head not relaxed and laid to the side on a cheek like a man sleeping but instead peering down. Rock as open space, veins of lighter stone like air curving around heavier stone, and the dead man might see into this world. A great lake at the center, molten and shifting, and all along the edges of this burning lake are beaches and islands, flatlands and mountains forming for a day or an instant and dissolved again, landscapes of impossible beauty never seen directly but only through density and mirage without air, and here the colonies of demons wait to rise through fissures and canals, pressed toward the surface, slipping along molten rips until they come closer and slow and finally are caged in hard stone, held forever just short of their desire, birthed only by the will of Satan, made of rock himself, half submerged, the one who would regress and recover and no longer deny. All forms are obedient to him. He has no fear and can take any shape. He looks only down. He knows that what happens anywhere above doesn't matter.

I enlarged the scab. That was all I could do. No shovel can dig through rock, just as no center of us can be reached or understood. We can only work away at the edges, chew away our own skin, and so I stabbed with that shovel in both hands like a knife plunging downward, on my knees before some sacrifice, and each stab went almost nowhere and I flung aside almost nothing.

My knees bitten into through my jeans, my hands blistering, the air thickening with day. The rock I uncovered was dark and ridged, weathered in some earlier time and then buried again.

One of the mountains near here submerged completely, buried under a plate and half burned, then returned to the surface again. Its rock half transformed and exposed now, showing us the underworld. Imagine that, an entire mountain gliding along and diving into the furnace, then rising out again quickly enough not to dissolve.

Nothing around us has ever been stationary. All of it is moving now, and all of it will be burned. It's an error to wonder when Satan might rise up. He's rising up now, the small stones falling away all along this ridge in piles of scree, that spine and goat's head freeing itself, already named, but all we might hear is a rock falling one night, and perhaps another rock the next year, and all we might see is nothing.

We won't see him rise, and neither will our children or our children's children or a hundred generations after, but some generation will know him as risen and gone wandering and will not be able to see Goat Mountain as it is now, all signs of it erased except a few small mounds disconnected. No one will imagine that they were once one mountain.

I removed all that would grow and all topsoil that would grow it, and the only part left of this shelf was under the dead man, so I stood uphill and put my toe under his ribs to turn him as my father had, but I was not strong enough. He was rubbery and the ends of him stayed where they were and his ribs sprang back.

So I knelt close on the downhill side and leaned over him. A hand at his armpit and another at his waist, and the maggots in close and surging, and I did not like this but I saw no other way. My face inches from him and the smell not what I had imagined. His earlier smell gone, taken by the maggots, and now he smelled almost like bread, or the wet dough of bread, yeasty and thick. The transformation into Communion, the body become bread and sustenance. Putrid, also, of course, but perhaps I was used to that, had been living in that smell, and the maggots really had made a change, and there was something milky, also, milk in a pail and the smell of udders. As if the dead man really would sustain us, as if that were his will. His intentions for us had never been clear.

I rolled him toward me, soft and heavy, his flesh feeling just like dough, and I might have been at some great table, and the maggots hidden against my knee now and his belly in close and I looked toward his face and he was looking down at me, benevolent. The most open expression, mouth loose and eyes gazing deep into mine and beyond and all relaxed, no more tricks, only sincerity. He was worried what would happen to us when he was gone.

I stared into those eyes. I couldn't look away. A different life to dead eyes, all fear gone, all reserve and calculation. A nakedness. An acceptance.

I knew now that we needed to give the dead man a proper burial. He needed a coffin to shield him from the dirt, so that those eyes could gaze always and be clear. It would be best if he could lie here on open ground, and even better if he could hang upside down again and look up into the heavens with those eyes that were limitless and might see even to the stars, but he needed to be protected, also. The thought of something ripping him into pieces was unbearable.

It's hard to know what the dead need or want. I had never heard the dead man's voice. Everything about him was only a rumor. If I had been there to know him alive, I'd know what to do now.

Tell me, I said. Tell me what to do.

It was then the sun hit, and this seemed a sign, but a sign of what? The warmth in my hair and I knelt over him and waited. The two of us on that narrow shelf on a steep slope, all fallen away around us, and I waited but the dead man did not speak. The sun only fell lower down my face and neck and chest, too hot and bright to look at, igniting welts of poison oak that had spread everywhere, and so I was scratching and my chin ducked like the dead man's and eyes squinting while his remained wide open.

My knees hurt in the rocks so I stood finally and grabbed the shovel, bent low and chopped at the area where he had lain. Stab and fling. The sound of rock and shovel, always dislocated, seeming to come from a few feet to the side, as if someone else were out here digging. Hinged shovel loose and worthless, dented and rusted at the edges and used in some war, burying the living as well as the dead.

I just kept digging, because I didn't know what else to do. I tried not to look at the dead man again, though he was constantly in the way, his feet and hands everywhere. I tried to take the entire area an inch deeper, kept hitting bedrock until I heard my father's footsteps above, rough slide of his boots.

He was bright in the sun, holding my rifle, coming down the glade fast, as if no step could ever fail. I had nearly forgotten him. And I looked down and realized that what I had dug here was not at all what he had wanted. What I had done didn't make any sense.

I couldn't do anything else, I said. It's all rock here.

My father charging still, unable to hear me, sliding and then quick steps to stop himself on this mound. His breath in jabs.

That's not a grave, he said.

It's all rock.

You owe that man a grave, and you had plenty of time.

We stood on either side of that body and the dead man made no comment. We needed my grandfather. He never hesitated, never seemed to hit a moment when all was unclear and no way forward.

My father leaned over and yanked the shovel from my hand. He gave me the rifle to hold, and I was happy to have it back. Reassuring weight, old steel.

My father stabbed at that mountain, and the mountain did not yield. A few small sparks, flint, as if he might find a fuse, but soon enough even those were erased by the sun and there was only the sound of metal striking stone.

Okay, my father finally said. Sweating in the sun, his T-shirt damp at the chest and his forehead wet. Okay.

He dropped the shovel and squatted low with his forearms on his knees. Looking down at the body. I wanted a burial, he said. Hiking on the ridge, I even felt a bit of hope. I thought maybe we'll leave this behind us. Give the man a decent burial and go home.

My father weak again. No anger, only sadness. I have sympathy for him now, and I wish I could go back, but I had no sympathy for him then. I stood removed on that raw patch of earth, and whatever closeness I had felt with the dead man I did not feel with my father.

Not a lot of options, my father finally said. And we need to end this.

My father stood then and grabbed the dead man's ankles and ran to the side and flung. It was so quick, I hardly saw it. I didn't get to say good-bye, didn't have a last look at his face. Sidesteps along the slope and my father just yanked the dead man into the air and then his pale body was scudding downward and stopped about fifteen feet below us, snagged on something, caught short.

Goddammit, my father said, and he slid down to the body and put both arms under and flung again and the dead man tumbled sideways, rolling faster and faster and gaining speed, pirouettes on a stage held sideways, and then he dove headfirst and planted his neck and the rest of him flipped over, a somersault, and landed hard and that's when the top half of him somehow came loose and soared into the air without the waist or legs. He had ripped in half at the cavern, freed now from all that would trouble him, and he was as graceful as any diver, arms out together and chin ducked and waiting for immersion. His work in this world complete.

Our camp at the lower end of the goat's rib cage, where he breathes. No Eden. This entire slope expanding and contracting, expanding and contracting. The enormous heart made of stone hidden away somewhere behind us under that ridge.

When we returned, my grandfather on his slab had his arms spread wide and mouth open, as if he would devour all, reclaim and ingest the world he had made, only borrowed by the rest of us. A great splitting sound from deep within him, shifting of continents, audible even over the truck.

Tom as far away as he could be, sitting in an old camp chair beyond the basin, facing us and my grandfather, not sleeping. His rifle across his knees.

My father turned off the truck and my grandfather's breath caught and it seemed almost that he might not breathe again, and I could hear only the water, but then he sucked in another great chunk of sky and the tumblers inside him ground again, chewing on rock and tree and cloud and returning each thing to what it was made of to be made again.

Is it done? Tom called out.

Yeah, my father said. He walked over to the table and I walked behind him with my rifle, keeping an eye on my grandfather and also on the buck's head where it hung now alone. Walking a kind of gauntlet between them. Antlers made larger by having no body. Head peering down but large eyes animated still. Something in them beyond what could be killed.

Where? Tom asked.

Upper glade.

Upper glade? How do you bury a man in the upper glade? That's a cliff with grass.

Well.

Well what? How the fuck did you bury him there?

My father sitting on the wrong side of the table, the downhill side, Tom's place. Tom standing now and pacing, holding his rifle in both hands like some wind-up soldier. He was always like this, guarding nothing, waiting for something but wholly unprepared, spooked from the moment I first pulled that trigger and spooked still, believing maybe everything was unreal and nothing had happened. He was like most people in that way. Continuing on, day to day and year to year, outraged and doing nothing.

Let's just have lunch, my father said, and

he didn't even look up. It wasn't a question. Because every Tom can be ignored. Tom didn't use his rifle but hung it over his shoulder on an old webbed strap, more army surplus, then opened one of his wooden boxes and began pulling out bread, lunch meat, cheese, mustard, ketchup, pickles, because that was what he did.

You didn't bury him there, Tom finally said.

In a way, my father said. It's done, anyway. An open-air burial.

As in no covering of dirt.

Yeah.

That kind of burial.

Yeah.

Well that'll look good.

No one's going to see it.

Won't they? Tom set down a paper plate with the lunch meat, perfect circles of flesh remade. Then he leaned in across the table, his face close to my father's. Listen, he said. Let's just leave right now. Before he wakes up. I'll say it was him. Even if it wasn't, it might as well have been. He's the one we have to watch out for. Tom glanced at me then, and he didn't seem entirely sure.

Stubble along Tom's cheeks and neck, dark stubble. Wearing no hat. Dark hair matted to his head. Those thick glasses and thin wire frames, eyes large and afraid.

Tom, my father said quietly. His face equally as stubbled and dirty, a vertical line in his cheek filled with dirt and sweat. The two of them peering at each other in close, humanity conspiring against their gods, against fate, ducked close in conference through every age, as if they could hide.

We just leave now, Tom whispered.

He's my father.

Save your son. That's enough. Someone doesn't make it out of this. There's no way around that.

Tom, you're not talking sense.

I'm the first one talking sense this entire trip. You listen, because this is the first time you've heard something that's not crazy.

My father shook his head and closed his eyes. He put his hands up over his face and rubbed at his forehead. The water in the basin a constant weight, and the stream beside us made of lead, pulling down this patch of earth and dragging it away. All of us holding on against that.

We just go back tomorrow, my father finally said. As we planned, and we move on. If we ever hear who the man was, we send something to his family to help them. Anonymous. And that's it.

Rivers of lead or mercury, heavy and

silver-gray, working down through this mountain, the arteries and veins. This entire ridge the buried goat made not of blood and flesh but of mercury and stone. I can't find the source of that pressure now, but it was always when I sat at that table, and perhaps it was only panic at how little held us together.

You think about this, Tom said. This is the rest of your life you're deciding right now.

It's already decided, my father said. There's nothing I can do. You and he both tell me to do things I can't do.

Tom bent down to pick something off the ground, something I couldn't see, but when he straightened, he had a small stone in his hand, and he hucked it at my grandfather where he slept. Rise and shine, fucker, he said. Looks like we're going on the hunt after all.

Aborted snore, half a lung sucked into his throat and blown back. Smacking sounds then, chewing on some meal from dreams, first images of what the world might be, and then an enormous yawn.

We all waited unmoving. The trees not pillars but ribs, this place not a cathedral but a cavern, and my grandfather was held nowhere. He was both smaller and larger than this mountain.

He bent his knees in the air, wearing only

his boxers, legs thin as bone, draped with loose pale skin and no meat, and he swung them forward to rise to a sitting position. Hundreds of pounds somehow levered by nothing at all. Only boxers, naked otherwise, and the great teats hanging down, pink and waiting to feed all that would be.

You look like deer, he said. Frozen in place, watching, about to jump.

Fuck that, Tom said. I'm not afraid of you.

My grandfather smiled.

Tom looked away, then sat down and started making a sandwich. My father and I unfroze and worked on our own sandwiches. The water thickening and slowing beside us. Pink meat and yellow cheese, white bread, red ketchup. All of us aware of every movement my grandfather made, pulling on his pants and boots, his shirt and jacket, tottering off to the outhouse and returning with his vacant stare to sit on the uphill bench beside Tom and swing his legs in. He reached for his knife, drove it into wood to stand beside our knives, large curved blades, and in this moment we could have been all the same, but only in this moment.

I see you decided not to use the buck's head, my grandfather said. So the man has had a proper burial?

My father glanced at me and didn't answer.

The two of us on the downhill side sharing a bench, hanging on.

Something went wrong, my grandfather said. I'm curious now.

I focused on chewing. The bread gumming at the roof of my mouth.

Well? he asked.

But my father only ate.

Did he come back to life? Was that the problem? Did you lose track of him?

My father brushed the crumbs off his hands, grabbed his knife and sheathed it, then stood. I'm leaving for the hunt in five minutes, he said. I don't care who's left behind.

Tom grabbed his knife and looked at my grandfather. Then he sheathed it and stood and walked away toward the truck. I'm ready, he said. His rifle already slung over his shoulder, and I saw he had his canteen, too.

What was it like to bury your kill? my grandfather asked me.

I didn't, I said.

So he's not buried?

No.

My grandfather smiled. Where is he, then?

In the upper glade. In two pieces. He fell apart.

Fell apart.

Yeah.

My grandfather grabbed his knife and

looked at it. He was chuckling. Fell apart.

It looked like he was taking a dive.

Into what?

I don't know.

My grandfather's pig eyes cold and small. The chuckling and grin on the surface only. The rest of us here for his grim entertainment. Holding his knife in one meaty fist, point up, twisting it slowly as if gouging the air, working a small rip, tearing a bit at the fabric of the air, opening some vacuum invisible that would begin to pull all things inward. Annihilation. It was always what my grandfather promised, and it might begin in one tiny point, without warning. He had a different relation to air and light and sound and weight. He was nimble even in the places we could not see.

Long curve of that blade, beveled to an edge too slight to know. Milky thickness beyond the bevel, metal polished so smooth it might have been liquid, pewter gray, associated with the mercury running through the veins of this mountain, similar satiny surface and unfathomable weight beneath.

A trick of my grandfather's to distract. Each of us lost, over and over.

The knife suddenly gone below the table, sheathed. And then he shifted his great bulk, swung his legs over the bench, and wandered off returned to nothing at all, a heap of flannel and wool.

My father had already started the truck. Sitting in the cab with Tom. Last hunt. The two staring ahead past the stream and water-wheels into the hillside, waiting.

The buck waiting also, slow revolution of blue-green galaxies at the back of those eyes, beyond annihilation. The rip my grandfather had opened might pull all things toward it but those eyes. Impulse and source.

This camp no refuge. It was not possible for us to carve out any place of our own. I understand that now. The stream and ferns and trees no barrier against the open meadow beyond or the mountain above, no separation.

My grandfather grabbed his .308 and stuffed into the cab, the truck dipping on that side, hanging tilted, and I waited until his door was closed, then passed and climbed the bumper.

My father backed and turned and we rumbled onto the road again, and I didn't know where we were headed. A hunt an evasion, an attempt to stall everything else.

The air ten degrees hotter the moment we left the trees. The sun bright off the top of the cab, and I was squinting. Usually the afternoon hunt was later, when the sun was lower. Everything off balance this trip. My father and I were supposed to have taken a nap, but all my father wanted now was movement.

Each tree trapped in its own heavy shadow, pinned down. Every open area blasted and washed out in white. Grasshoppers flung like small rocks heated until they popped. Dragonflies cruising on solar wings.

I tried to look for bucks, but a buck here would be no more than a mirage. Shadow form stamped into the white and then fading almost instantly. Thrum of cicadas over-whelming, rubbing at the air and dissolving shape, making it nearly impossible to see.

White manzanita, each bush of it a thou-sand velvety mirrors, arrayed on both sides of the road, hung separate from the earth, wink-ing among green manzanita with leaves almost as bright. Their only intent confusion. The road lost somewhere in that maze.

We fell into the draw below the reservoir, and the leaves of the wild grape had all fused into one brightness, hot mantle of a lantern flung and grown. Shade then, and my eyes with no time to adjust before we emerged in light again, and we passed the road to bear wallow. My father driving us on.

No blue to this sky. All blue burned away. Heat waves risen over the blackened arms of fallen ponderosa pines, melting in waves amid dry brown sedge. Thick clumps of it on all sides, resisting erasure, spiking through the melt. The road before us a memory of water, dry now but rutted with scabs grown inward.

Falling downward always, this road the beginning of what would become a canyon, our stamp left on the earth. And my father took the next turnoff, a little-used track overgrown with thistle purple and green amid the brown, a road leading to the burn, the lowest section of the ranch where a wildfire had swept through and laid waste to all. A place where the ground itself was red and black as if still on fire and might cave away beneath you as you walked. False diamonds there, clear shards and chips as thick as your finger lying everywhere on the surface, as if all might be given, formed under pressure in some earlier time and now simply offered up.

Forked ridges braced against the valley below, Satan's hoof, leverage for his rise. We stood at the top of that fork, the four of us at the edge, a place soundless except for the rise of air from that superheated ground, dark bare surface armored in exposed black rock.

Charred skeletons of every tree and bush twisting below us. Manzanita in blackened baskets reaching upward, oak branches burrowing sideways through the air, tips whitened, no green, no leaves. All seeming to writhe, still in motion. We stood at the tip of the flame, both slopes curling inward orange and red like the surface of the sun drawn upward. Immolation if it weren't for time, and mirages still boiling.

Something red to that ground, small bits of red rock or something transformed, no vein of it or anything solid, and maybe it was only the red of the manzanita, some sheen to that even when dead or dormant, changing the light.

Snake, Tom said, and then I saw it, not twenty feet away downslope, coiled behind a dark stump of ruined buckbrush. Fat and slack, deflated against the ground, light brown diamonds all along it, rattles up but motionless, still considering, head levered just enough in the air to flick that tongue and smell.

At the end of a hunt, we would have shot it, but not the beginning. All deer would instantly be gone.

Fucker thinks he can take us, my father said. Not even sure we're worth the effort.

Dry dull skin of the snake. Shadow so black, so sharp and thin along the borders he seemed separate from the ground, not touching. The flattening of him a lie, flattened against nothing. He might reappear anywhere along this slope. And I began to see the buck-brush beside him the same, shadowed at the surface and no roots below, the entire black slope a hard plate, impenetrable, and every object floating and shifting upon it.

No gravity here. Nothing to pull downward. An object might rise along the slope as well as fall. Hard to know which way we tilted. No direction, either, the sun directly above. A compass would only spin.

My grandfather stepped onto that slope and seemed to hang at right angles to it, moving fast, and the snake uncoiled, long slack rope fleeing without challenge or rattle or even much of a curve, flown almost in a straight panicked line, an S no more than memory, and the rough sound of its heavy body rubbing against the earth a memory also, dragging of scales already gone. It knew what to fear.

My grandfather's boots now where the snake had lain, and he peered up at us looking for reaction, face buried in shadow beneath his cap, bulk erased by that enormous hunting jacket, rifle strapped over his shoulder. I stood there in full sweat in that heat, my entire body slick, and he made no sense to me.

The three of us against him, but there was nothing substantial in us. We were made of nothing.

You're a crazy fuck, Tom finally said. I'll give you that.

My grandfather expressionless, waiting, but waiting for what?

Just go on your hunt, my father said.

My grandfather become one of the burned trees, only another shape that might slide along the surface of that slope. What I saw was him biting a giant chunk out of rock and speaking at us in crushed bits of stone, but what happened was that he dropped to his knees, mouth open in a rough grunt of pain, then rolled over and sat facing downslope, taking the seat of the snake.

I was encased in poison oak now, red welts everywhere across my body on fire, a burning thing, layers of immolation: my skin, the boils and welts, my clothing, the superheated air. Even my sweat a kind of oil ignited.

I guess I'll go down and flush out any bucks, Tom said. Since no one else seems ready to do anything.

Fair enough, my father said, and Tom went down that tilted slope and gave my grandfather wide berth. Footsteps that left no mark. A surface that could not be broken. Tom wearing camouflage green in a place where there was no green, and yet that place swallowed him anyway, dark green against black. Angling off to the right and the hillside growing as he became smaller. My father and I sat at the lip, uphill of my grandfather, keeping him in view.

Pointless, my father said. You won't be able to hit anything that far away with a .30–.30, and I don't even have a gun.

My grandfather with his .308 across his knees, sitting cross-legged now.

Tom changed course, cut to his left into the center of the draw, where great boulders had fallen or been exposed and a large stand of pine waited, trunks blackened and become white-gray above, dead sentinels with bare arms and no heads.

He's going for cover, my grandfather said.

What? my father asked.

He's running, and he's going for cover, those pine snags and boulders and falls. He can find cover most of the way down.

You're crazy, just like he said.

My grandfather raised his rifle to his shoulder, aiming downslope, braced his elbows on his knees in firing position.

What are you doing? my father asked. His voice quiet, dry, and I was holding my breath, waiting for the explosion. My grandfather capable of anything.

I can see him in the scope. He's taking glances up here and moving fast. He's running. He wouldn't be looking up here if he was hunting.

He's just flushing bucks.

Nope. And he's still close enough. Not more than two hundred and fifty yards. Still big enough in the scope.

Big enough for what?

You knew there was going to be consequence. You knew that all along.

My father raised his hands to his mouth and blew, the call of an owl, his signature. We waited, and we heard the hollow sound of Tom's answering call float up toward us. See? He's just flushing bucks.

He's heading down to the valley, where

he'll hitch a ride or just keep walking, and he's going to report all that we've done. We're going to swing, our entire family, because you didn't do what you needed to. Because you're weak and you refuse to see what's coming.

My grandfather still aiming at Tom through that scope. Tom threading down through the snags.

You're not pulling that trigger. My father's hand on my .30–.30, taking it from me quietly.

You're right. Your son is going to pull the trigger.

The entire mountainside below moving toward me, ridges curling back, a rushing sound in my head. The skin of the earth stretching. We called it buck fever. Blindness, loss of hearing, heart clenching as if it would rip itself free, surge of each pump through arteries yanking stumps of legs and arms. The pure thrill of killing, even more magnificent when it's a man and not an animal. Adrenaline. A surge within that takes us all the way back, before Jesus, before the written word or even the spoken word, before we think of ourselves as being, before we walk upright, before we enter this world as anything that can be called us, this surge when we kill, mark of Cain before there is even an idea of Cain or the possibility of Abel. That heart yanking is truth.

My father slumped over beside me, broken. He would not stop this. I knew that. His head between his knees, rifle low in both hands, resting on his boots. His eyes closed. Same surge in him, and felt as ruin.

Come down here, my grandfather said, but I could not move. I could hardly breathe.

You don't want me to come get you, he said.

My hands braced on rock to either side so that I would not fall, and even rock was caving away. My grandfather had paralyzed us both. It was not possible to run from him. I could only watch as he rose on those spindles and the earth swung but he remained upright.

I don't know what to call him now. Beyond any name. He rose toward me the same as law, as whatever made adrenaline. As close as I can know to the creation itself, and he grabbed the top of my head, fingers clenched in my hair, and dragged me down that slope face-first.

Torn across black scab and outcrop, glittering of Lake County diamonds emerged from nowhere, lying on the surface, and no ash. No ash anywhere, all blown and gone, but a thousand blackened seeds and bits of bark and stone. Carried and I might have been carried forever, facedown to see all, every landscape and what it held or might become.

Brought to where the snake had coiled, dropped and then yanked upright into a sitting position and the rifle in my hands.

Shoot him, my grandfather said.

Rifle I had never held before, a kind of sacrament, dark oiled wood and black bolt, black scope. Knees up in a wide base and my elbows braced on them, and the stock in tight against my shoulder, all unthinking, all trained for as many years as I had memory. Aiming without the scope first, as I'd been taught, sighting a landmark, a large snag, then finding this in the scope and shifting downward to find Tom.

Tom in the crosshairs, hustling over rocky ground, hopping as if his feet were on fire, getting close to that snag and a large boulder, cover. The scope shrinking and flattening the world. That boulder could have been five feet past him or twenty-five feet. The way my grandfather saw us always, magnified and up close and distances gone and always seeing our backs, running away.

Every jigsaw piece of camouflage on Tom's back sharp and clear, and the scope hovering around him, shaken by each pump of blood.

Shoot him, my grandfather said, and I held

my breath, pulled that rifle in tight, but I did not want to kill. I was done with killing.

Shoot him. My grandfather's hand on the back of my neck, ready to crush or twist and snap. Fingers rough as scales.

I timed the hovering of the scope and pulled softly on that trigger just as the crosshairs swung across Tom's back, but I closed my eyes, also, and flinched.

The concussion and hard insistence of the rifle, taste of sulfur, and though it wasn't the .300 magnum, it was still much more powerful than the .30–.30, and my shoulder and back were instantly stunned. I knew this but didn't feel it. The adrenaline muting all. What I saw was a puff against the boulder beyond Tom, rock pulverized into dust, like some meteor hitting, dust unexpectedly white coming from blackened rock.

Tom's arms went up instinctively, as if the sky were falling, and he ran now, full tilt, bent over low and holding his rifle in one hand.

You kill him or I kill you, my grandfather said. Taking a shot is not enough. You keep your eyes open, and you make the next one count.

I pulled back the bolt and levered a new shell, but now Tom was behind the snag, black pine charred and rutted. He stood behind that trunk and held his barrel pinned against it, an excellent brace, and we heard his bullet slam into the ground below us before we heard the crack.

Shoot him.

Let him kill us, my father said. That's the best thing. Just stand up and wait.

I looked back over my shoulder and my father was standing at the edge with his arms out, the .30–.30 abandoned at his feet. His white shirt an easy target.

Life was wasted on you, my grandfather said.

Then take it back, my father said. I won't be this.

A spout of earth beside me, another bullet hitting and somehow creating this dust from what I had thought was rock. A venting. A way in.

I put my hand out to feel the crust. Platelets broken free. Formed by water and fire, all that had dissolved hardened again, the making of new rock.

My hand jumping from that ground, taken on its own life, and I had been shot. A hole through the back of my hand, blood everywhere, and the pain hot, searing hot, as if blood were fire.

My father screaming. Shoot me, you stupid fuck! Leave my son alone!

My hand against the dirt, and I didn't

understand. Two bullets in exactly the same place. It seemed inevitable there would be a third, that another bullet would go through the hole in my hand and into this vent, guided by something more than we know.

My grandfather grabbed the top of my head and pointed me downslope. Focus, he said.

The pain gathered in my skull. Leaking from my hand into the liquid space around my brain, molten.

My grandfather slapped me. Stay awake, he said. Get those crosshairs on him.

I put my cheek against the stock and found Tom in that scope. I could see him reloading, gun held downward, slipping rounds into its underside. Only his hands visible, one foot, part of a shoulder, dark as shadow.

I can't shoot him, I said. I can't shoot Tom. You will.

The center of the crosshairs swimming drunkenly over Tom and that tree, the blood pulsing and my breath ragged. He raised his rifle, taking a sidestep, exposed, and I pulled the trigger and thought he would be dead. His body folded and thrown, this is what I would see through the scope, my own doing, and the look of surprise on his face, like the dead man, an unwillingness to believe.

But the bullet was swallowed somewhere

without sign, taken away and vanished, as if it had never been fired, and I imagined I was immune, that no bullet could come from me again.

Tom fired. I could see that in the scope, and instantly my leg was ripped. I looked down and saw two holes in my jeans, my right thigh, blood already and a dull ache and the world shuttering.

The black of this ground become the air. My grandfather slapping me again, shaking me. My father screaming, a sound small and muffled and far away and meaningless.

My grandfather whispering in my ear. I will cut open every part of you. I will peel away strips until you cover the ground all the way from here to there. I will undo every part that was made.

The smell from inside him, the heat of him, and I knew that he would pull me apart with his bare hands and snap through bone and think nothing of it. In every memory he was there, waiting, annihilation and source.

He pulled the bolt and loaded the last shell as I held the rifle. You make this one count, he said.

So I raised that rifle into the sky and pulled the trigger, and the butt was not close against my shoulder so it slammed into my chest and knocked me down.

275

My grandfather's hand over my face, fingers squeezing at the edges of my eyes. All of this comes from you, he said. From what you did. This is the consequence, and you will finish what you owe.

His fingers pressing in, and I was terrified I'd lose my eyes, the fear jolting me awake. I couldn't see, but I swung at him with my good hand.

That's right, he said. You shoot him or I take out your eyes.

A terrible god. That's all we know. Atavistic fear. God that would make us and destroy us, but we've forgotten this god. Our dreams of Jesus have made us soft.

My grandfather pressed me flat against that black earth and was ready to take my eyes. That's what I know. The mass of him, heavier than this mountain, a different gravity. All that we fail to believe.

Pressing me down through crust, toward the inferno, all of me on fire. But then he held my head in both hands, as if he would care for me. And he was smiling. He was curious about my pain. Unconcerned about bullets coming our way.

You will kill, he said. Eyes gray and small and empty in their centers. Eyes made of time, threads in that gray streaming outward from darkness, bundles and cords of light begun invisible, appearing at the inner edge and crossing that ring to vanish again at the outer edge. The gray a kind of pearl, the surface no surface at all. I was sinking beneath those threads into others beneath, galaxies opening, bundles of pearl-gray cord infinite and revealed only here. I could fall through this place, fall through time, and there would be no end, no ground.

All that is terrible is beautiful. And the times we see are always too brief. A bullet tore into the back of my left leg, deep into the muscle, lodged in bone. No graze but a falling away of breath and thought and the spread of some deep animal fear. I closed my eyes and my grandfather sat me upright, shook me and braced a knee behind my back. The rifle in my hands, and he was sliding in another round.

You will kill him now, he said. You will find him in that scope and feel those crosshairs dig into his chest and let that bullet go. You will do that or you will die here.

I could no longer speak. I was falling away and my grandfather was keeping me from falling. I looked through the scope and saw empty sky, whited blue. Then trees from the mountains far on the other side of the valley rushing at impossible speeds, flung across the surface in arcs, then black ground, white twisted shapes, and my leg was hollowed out and burning, a kind of shell for holding flame.

My father had come closer. Somehow I knew that. An ally. My grandfather rising up like some great bear to meet him, and I knew he would crush my father. Skull in his hands. I fell back against the earth and he blotted out most the sky, becoming larger in every moment, feeding on our fear, and I swung that rifle upward and leaned the barrel against his side and pulled the trigger.

The boom in close, odd muffled sound with the barrel against him, and I knew the shot would have no effect. He was too large, growing still, and he was made of something we've never known, something that pulls against all else we can see or feel and makes its birth possible, something that can bring rock itself into being. This bullet would travel endlessly inside him and never find a target. It would travel for thousands of years and hit nothing because it would have a shadow somewhere immovable. Those thousands of years become less than an instant and the bullet vanished and winking into being and gone.

Dark sky above me swaying in place, and some vent had been opened. I heard his lung collapse, heard the breath of it come out through his side, and it seemed almost that he could be a man. My own head swimming, riding waves of pain and pulse, blacking out, but I could see him turn and look down at me and his mouth was open for air. No intake, and there was amazement on his face.

He looked at me as if I were god myself, his final trick.

His arms and hands shrunken away and reaching for me. He was tottering backward, righted himself, tilted forward, and I knew he would fall and I would be crushed.

His eyes the brightest gray, brushed metal, and fixed on me as his enormous bulk came down. A fall we took together, meeting somewhere between, time slowed and gravity thinned, and what I felt was love.

That fall an eternity, and I was crushed between mountains, held against black earth by the weight of something darker still, and had no breath. My father's face lost and desperate, made a child again, pulling at the great body, all his world gone. He pulled at that body until it was rolled off me, and then he wept over his father.

It was not possible for my grandfather to die. He broke every rule when he did that. God without end.

I'd like to thank the John Simon Guggenheim Memorial Foundation and the University of San Francisco for generous support during the writing of this novel, and Colm Tóibín, Janet Burroway, and David Kirby for recommending me.

I'd also like to thank everyone at Heinemann, especially Jason Arthur and Emma Finnigan, and my UK agent Peter Straus and film agent Rob Kraitt at Casarotto Ramsay & Associates in addition to everyone at Inkwell in the US.

And of course I must thank John L'Heureux and Michelle Carter, because this novel returns to the material of the first short story I ever wrote, more than twenty-five years ago. This is the novel that burns away the last of what first made me write, the stories of my violent family. It also reaches back to my Cherokee ancestry, faced with the problem of what to do with Jesus.

WALK A NARROW MILE

Faith Martin

Ex-DI Hillary Greene, now working as a consultant to the cold-case team of the Thames Valley Police, is still traumatized by a vicious attack from a stalker who, it now appears, was responsible for a string of other cases involving missing girls. Her bosses are worried she is not up to the job — and Hillary, too, suffers despair at her failure to make progress and catch the man who might not be content the next time simply to leave her with one scar to remember him by . . .

THE GHOSTS OF MAYFIELD COURT

Norman Russell

July, 1894. When Maximilian Paget inherits Mayfield Court, he and his niece Catherine find it to be half-ruined and haunted by the wraith of a murdered child. Catherine discovers a child's skeleton, bringing rural Detective Inspector Jackson and his bibulous but shrewd sergeant, Herbert Bottomley, to investigate. Once returned to London, neither uncle nor niece can shake off the baleful influence of Mayfield. And when Uncle Max is murdered by a deranged killer who, Jackson discovers, has left a trail of corpses in an attempt to secure a hidden fortune, Catherine herself faces imminent death, and a monstrous betrayal . . .

DEATH IN TRANSIT

Keith Moray

West Uist, Scotland. When a body is found floating in Kyleshiffin harbour, it is unclear whether there has been a tragic accident or a cold-blooded murder. A chalked astrological sign on the harbour wall gathers significance when a second body and another sign are discovered. This time there is no doubt — it was murder most foul. There is no shortage of suspects, with tensions running high between the local astronomical and astrological societies. And the signs are that there will be more deaths, unless Inspector Torquil McKinnon and his team can solve the case and find the zodiac killer.

THE HEALER

Antti Tuomainen

It's three days before Christmas, and Helsinki is battling remorseless flooding and disease. Social order is crumbling and private security firms have undermined the police force. Tapani Lehtinen, a struggling poet, is among the few still willing and able to live in the city. When his wife Johanna, a journalist, goes missing, he embarks on a frantic hunt for her. Johanna's disappearance seems to be connected to a story she was researching about a politically motivated serial killer known as 'The Healer'. Determined to find Johanna, Tapani's search leads him to uncover secrets from her past: secrets that connect her to the very murders she was investigating . . .

KILLER IN BLACK

Paul Bennett

In a small town in Texas, five ex-mercenaries reunite when one of their number, Red — half-Comanche, half-Texan — is threatened. The town's sheriff won't risk his job by helping, so it's down to Johnny Silver and his band of comrades to sort the matter out. The resultant attacks escalate from a simple poisoning of a ranch's water supply, to full-scale war with a fifty-strong gang of bikers. And pulling the strings is their most formidable foe yet — a professional assassin, the Killer in Black. Is Johnny's team still strong enough to take on the challenges posed by their enemy? Or have they finally met their match?

DEATH WARMED UP

John Paxton Sheriff

Jack Scott and Sian Laidlaw are forced to remain in Gibraltar with Jack's mother after she breaks her ankle. When a chance meeting with a young photographer, Pru Wise, leads them into the path of trouble and up against a ruthless diamond robber, it becomes clear that there are some dangerous forces at work. Then the dead body of Pru turns up in the boot of a car registered to Sian . . . In order to unravel a web of intrigue, the duo must face a violent climax in the house of an ex-diplomat, and survive a fight to the death on the rocks of Gibraltar's most southerly shore.